SPARKLING NEW

FROM PRIZE-WINNING AUTHORS

# Mirrors

First published in Great Britain by Collins in 2001
First published in paperback by Collins in 2002
Collins is an imprint of HarperCollins*Publishers* Ltd
77-85 Fulham Palace Road, Hammersmith, London W6 8JB

The HarperCollins website address is www.**fire**and**water**.com

1 3 5 7 9 8 6 4 2

The Fateful Mirror © Elizabeth Laird 2001
The Mirrored Garden © Gaye Hiçyilmaz 2001
mirror dot com © Lesley Howarth 2001
Never Trust a Parrot © Jeremy Strong 2001
Watching © Oneta Malorie Blackman 2001
Selim-Hassan the Seventh © Vivian French 2001
Whose Face do you See? © Melvin Burgess 2001
Silver Laughter © Celia Rees 2001
Use it or Lose It © Anne Fine 2001
Double Vision © Paul Stewart 2001
The Dragon's Dream © Kate Thompson 2001
Rochefault's Revenge © Alan Durant 2001
Lilac Peabody © Annie Dalton 2001
The Disappearance © Mary Arrigan 2001
The Girl of Silver Lake © Berlie Doherty 2001

Collection copyright © Wendy Cooling 2001
Illustrations by Sarah Young and Tim Stevens

ISBN 000 710589 4

The authors and editor assert the moral right to be
identified as the authors and editor of the work.

Printed and bound in Great Britain by
Omnia Book Manufacturing Ltd, Glasgow

SPARKLING NEW STORIES
FROM PRIZE-WINNING AUTHORS

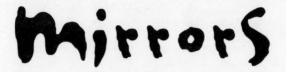

EDITED BY WENDY COOLING

ILLUSTRATIONS BY
SARAH YOUNG AND TIM STEVENS

*An imprint of* HarperCollins*Publishers*

*Also edited by Wendy Cooling*

CENTURIES OF STORIES
LISTEN TO ME!

# CONTENTS

# Introduction

**Mirrors** and reflections have played their part in stories from the ancient tales of the basilisk and the story of Snow White, to the present day story of Harry Potter. The mythical basilisk could turn a creature to stone with just a look and could only be destroyed by seeing its own reflection in a mirror. Snow White's step-mother appeals to her all-seeing mirror for confirmation of her beauty. Harry Potter finds the Mirror of Erised and sees in it what he desires most in life – his family.

The dictionary definition of 'mirror' is something that gives a faithful reflection. In fiction, mirrors do not have to play by the rules! This book contains fifteen newly written stories in which a mirror plays a vital part. One is a beautiful re-telling of the story of Narcissus and his reflection – perhaps the oldest mirror story of all – and the rest, brand new stories that reflect the imaginations of some of today's finest writers. Read the stories in any order, then maybe you'll want to go on and look at some of the novels written by these authors.

Enjoy!

Wendy Cooling

**Elizabeth Laird**

# THE FATEFUL MIRROR
*The Story of Echo and Narcissus*

**Illustration by Sarah Young**

*Elizabeth Laird*

## THE FATEFUL MIRROR
*The Story of Echo and Narcissus*

In ancient times, when the old gods ruled from Mount
Olympus, a handsome young hunter roamed the earth,
trapping in his nets any prey that came within his reach.

He was sixteen years old, and already many young
women, and men too, had fallen in love with him.

His name was Narcissus.

In the forest where he hunted, a young girl wandered,

looking for flowers. She talked as she ran about, and her tongue, like her feet, was never still. But her speech was meaningless, for the goddess Juno, angered by the girl's endless chatter, had cruelly condemned her only to repeat the words that others spoke.

Her name was Echo.

One day, worn out by the hunt, Narcissus lay down in the shade of a spreading tree and closed his eyes. Echo ran past and saw him. She stopped at once when she saw the boy, then crept towards him and stood looking down at him, at the dark curls falling over his high forehead, the blush of red on his cheek, and the slender strong hands that still held his nets as he slept. And as she gazed at him, she fell in love.

She longed to touch his hand, to wake him and tell him that she loved him, but she could not. The only words she could utter would be echoes of his own.

She crept away and hid behind a tree.

I'll wait, she thought. When he wakes up I'll follow him and listen. Perhaps he'll say something I can repeat, to show him that I love him.

At last Narcissus opened his eyes, sighed, sat up and stretched himself. Then he looked round. With the sharp senses of the hunter he knew he was not alone.

'Who's there?' he called out.

Echo trembled at the sound of his voice, lightly shaking the branch she was holding. The leaves rattled and a leaf fell to the ground.

'Who's there?' Narcissus called again.

He thought a wild animal must be lurking in the bushes, ready to leap out at him, so he snatched up his nets and ran forward to catch it. Echo stepped silently aside and hid herself under an overhanging rock.

Puzzled, Narcissus moved on through the forest and, flitting noiselessly from tree to tree, Echo followed him. Often he stopped and looked over his shoulder, and she froze in her tracks, so that in the dappled light that shone through the leaves overhead, he would mistake her for the trunk of a young sapling, or a shaft of light, shining on a boulder.

All day she followed him, waiting for her chance, her heart brimming over with love and longing.

At last, when the sun was setting, Narcissus stopped. He could no longer ignore the uneasy prickling in his neck, that told him by his hunter's instinct that he was being followed.

'Whoever you are,' he called out angrily, 'show yourself! Come here!'

'Come here!' answered Echo, taking her chance, and summoning all her courage, she stepped out into the open and ran up to him, her eyes soft with adoration.

Narcissus stepped back.

'What's this? Who are you?' he said.

'Who are you?' repeated Echo, letting her voice linger on the final word.

She stepped near to him, but dazzled by his beauty did not notice the cold disdain in his eyes.

'Stop! Don't touch me!' cried Narcissus.

'Touch me!' laughed Echo, delighted that at last the words she was forced to say reflected her true feelings, and she tried to throw her arms round his neck.

Narcissus pushed her roughly aside. He had never known love, and he had none to give.

'What are you doing?' he shouted angrily. 'How dare you think that I could love you?'

'I could love you,' faltered Echo, her eyes filling with tears.

'Go away. Leave me alone,' Narcissus said, and he turned on his heel and walked away.

'Away! Alone!' murmured Echo.

Her face burned with shame and she slipped back into the shadow of the trees. Rejected, her heart shrinking with misery, she fled from the forest, and wandering aimlessly, took refuge in the cold, distant mountains. There she starved herself, refusing to eat, and at last she pined away, until all that remained of her was her voice.

Down in the forest, the spirits of the woods and the water were angry with the cold-hearted Narcissus. They held up their hands to heaven and called out, 'Gods, punish Narcissus! Let him love, but never be loved in return.'

Nemesis, the god of vengeance, heard their prayers. He began to watch Narcissus, waiting for the chance to punish him.

One day, hot and tired after a weary hunt, Narcissus stumbled into a forest clearing, where reeds and lush marsh flowers grew up around the rim of a woodland pool. He knelt beside the water and lowered his head, ready to drink. But then, shimmering beneath him, the image of a face seemed to rise up through the water and gaze at him.

The face was framed with black curls that fell across a pale forehead. A pair of eyes, dark in their sockets and full of wonder, looked into his. Beneath the nose, straight and perfectly formed, the red lips were parted in surprise.

Enchanted, Narcissus stared. The creature in the water was the loveliest thing he had ever seen, and his heart was filled with the first passionate love he had ever known.

Trembling, he put out his hand, longing to touch and stroke the creature's soft cheek. But as soon as his hand touched the water, the lovely face disappeared, fractured by a thousand ripples.

Afraid he had been too hasty, Narcissus shrank back, then slowly, his heart beating fast, he leaned forward again.

The face had returned. Almost faint with relief, Narcissus cried out with joy. The lips below him parted soundlessly, as if the image was answering his delight.

'Who are you?' whispered Narcissus. 'A nymph?'

The mouth beneath him moved, silently giving back the question.

'I love you! Oh, I love you!' cried Narcissus.

Slowly, carefully, he lowered his face to the water. The image rose to meet him. The eyes gazed worshipfully into his. The mouth was pursed to kiss.

Narcissus shut his eyes, and his head was spinning as he bent lower still, longing to feel the soft lips on his own.

Instead of warm flesh he touched cold water.

His eyes flew open. The face had splintered again into jagged shards of light. He could see nothing but a writhing nose, shaking shadows where the eyes should be, and a broken mouth that twisted and disappeared, then formed itself again and gaped in horror that echoed his own.

Filled with despair, Narcissus lay down on the bank again and wept.

It was evening now, and a little breeze ruffled the water. Leaves blew down on to its surface, and fish leaped up from the depths to snatch at the gnats that hovered over the shimmering pool. Narcissus gazed and gazed, but the creature he loved had gone.

'I'll stay here,' Narcissus whispered to the pool. 'I'll wait and watch till you return, and then I'll love you forever.'

He slept when darkness fell. In the morning, the breeze had dropped and an early mist covered the water. Anxiously, Narcissus waited, and as it cleared the face appeared to him again.

Narcissus greeted it rapturously and pleaded with his loved one to step out of the water and embrace him, but the cold image only moved silently in reply.

In desperation, Narcissus called out, 'I know you love me as much as I love you. You stretch out your arms and raise your lips to kiss me whenever I lower mine. You laugh when I laugh, and your sighs are the same as mine. Only a little stretch of water keeps us apart, but it could be the widest ocean or the deepest river because however much I try I can never cross it.'

His tears fell then and disturbed the water, and his reflection shattered and disappeared.

'Where are you going, my love? Come back! Don't leave me!' he called out in despair.

A kind of madness had seized Narcissus. Unable to tear himself away from the pool, he no longer ate or drank, and he began to waste away, worn out by love. His dark curls hung limply round his face. His cheeks grew pale and thin. His arms could no longer lift the nets which he had once hurled so skilfully to trap the running deer. His legs had no strength now to support him.

He could only lie and gaze at himself, and he became weaker and weaker, day by day.

Echo heard his despairing cries, and her soft voice repeated them, sending them sadly through the forest clearing, her distress matching his own.

At last, exchanging one final long look with his own reflection, Narcissus murmured, 'My only love, goodbye!' And he closed his eyes and died.

'Goodbye!' Echo whispered, and the surface of the pool shivered as the sound of her voice rippled over it.

On the heights of Mount Olympus, the gods grieved for the handsome boy who now lay dead by the pool. They changed him into a flower. And if you, who are reading this story, should roam through the woods in the springtime, and if you should come to a pool in a clearing between the trees, you will find narcissus flowers growing at the water's edge, their white petals perfectly reflected in the cold clear water.

And if you should then climb up to the wild high places, or down to the sea where the cliffs rear up from the shore, or into the caves that tunnel the hills, and if you should call out, raising your own voice, 'Hello! Are you there?' Echo will hear you. Echo will answer, repeating the words, 'You there!'

You will call out again, and she will answer again, and again, her restless soul calling out to you, on and on to the end of time.

*Gaye Hiçyılmaz*

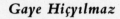

# THE MIRRORED GARDEN

*Illustration by Sarah Young*

*Gaye Hiçyılmaz*

## THE MIRRORED GARDEN

I first saw the mirrored garden on my way back from the beach. I hadn't even wanted to go to the seaside last year, and I'd told them so, but they hadn't taken any notice of that.

'Rubbish,' Dad had said challengingly. 'You'll love it.'

'Never mind, Chris,' Dad's girlfriend, Lizzie, was more honest. 'It's only a week. It'll pass in a flash and there's loads to do at the sea.'

'Like what?' I demanded. 'Going on donkey rides?'

Lizzie had shrugged and looked at Dad with her jelly brown eyes.

'Or making sand castles,' I persisted, but I didn't remind her that I was fourteen and not into buckets and spades. She didn't remind me that she was twenty-one and not into being anyone's mother, let alone mine.

Lizzie and I were as careful of each other as brain surgeons confronted by an unexpected lump.

'What's wrong with sand castles?' Dad asked. 'I used to love that beach at your age. People made brilliant things with sand.'

'Sure!' I quipped. 'Like concrete.'

'That's not what I meant. I meant sand sculptures, and...' Dad isn't into arty things but he tried, because he knew I was. 'And sand pictures and...'

'Wow.'

Dad swallowed. Lizzie shrugged again. She blinked slowly, like a lizard in the sun, then went into their room to pack their bags.

'It's OK,' I shrugged as well. 'I'm *going*, aren't I?'

'You certainly are!' Dad was brisk although his glance was anxious.

My friend Stubby was unsympathetic too. He said that family visits were rarely fatal, and never in a week, but he did agree they were a dreadful bore.

Stubby was wrong. We all were. It *was* boring. It was boring like I've never known boring could be, but I didn't die. I didn't even sicken. I loved it. I sucked up each gently stretched-out minute and rolled it round my tongue. The boredom was as delicious and chewy as those 2p sweets I used to buy at the newsagent's on my way home from school, and I wanted more.

It was years since I'd actually seen my grandparents: well, three and a half, to be exact. They mentioned this the moment I got off the train. It was awkward. I hung my head and muttered the dreaded word *divorce*. I always do that in tight spots. People shut up straight away. They didn't. They shook their grey heads and laughed. It wasn't Mum and Dad's divorce that had stopped them from visiting. It was the *dog,* Jasper. Jasper had a bad heart now, and other problems.

He didn't look like he had a bad heart, but he was big. In fact, when Gran opened the front door and we had all clambered over him, I appreciated their point of view. Jasper was gigantic. If *he* hadn't found the three flights of stairs up to Dad's flat a problem, the stairs definitely might. I've made them creak and I'm not huge at all.

Later, as I was edging round the bed in the tiny spare room and wondering how to unpack, Grandpa called out. I left my bag on the bed and hurried down, but Jasper had beaten me to it. He was flopped out in the sitting room, drooling chocolate on to the carpet and looking pretty satisfied with life.

The odd thing was, that I was happy too. Even after I'd noticed that the family photos on the mantelpiece were all of Jasper, I wasn't put out. I examined them with Gran. We admired Jasper as a pup in his basket, as a young dog with a big stick, and in massive middle age, with a loud tartan collar, and I didn't mind at all.

'He's done all right,' Gran folded her arms and smiled to herself. Grandpa nodded and I nodded too. Fleetingly, I remembered Dad in his new black jeans, with Lizzie at his side.

'Come on then, lad.' Grandpa had suddenly got up. I jumped to my feet, expecting a walk down to the sea or at least a tour of his greenhouse, but he turned his back.

'It's only Jasper,' Gran confided as the dog lumbered past. 'He's got to be reminded to spend a penny now.'

'Oh.' I was glad they hadn't visited. Old dogs wouldn't have been Lizzie's thing at all.

That evening Gran turned up the TV, then fell asleep. Grandpa went in and out with Jasper and that was it. Sometimes Gran snuffled and woke up to watch a bit, and sometimes Jasper snored, but nobody spoke to me at all.

It was such a relief. Nobody noticed me and I hardly knew I was there.

I had cornflakes for breakfast then a small white egg like a stone. When I'd made my bed, I cleaned my teeth with care. I even combed my hair. As I came down Gran was at the bottom of the stairs.

'I've made fish paste and jam.' She was holding up a polythene bag of neat, white sandwiches, with the crusts cut off. Jasper sulked. 'And I've put in squash. You like squash, don't you, Chris?'

'Actually—'

'Good. I thought you would. Now dear, don't hurry back. We know what young people are like.'

'I—'

'We don't have supper till six. After Jasper's had his. So 'bye dear, until then.'

I was so surprised I tripped on the step.

I didn't head for the beach, but kept it for last, like the crispiest bite of a Chinese. Killing time, I idled along the silent, neatly gardened street and on into town. A sea breeze swung B&B signs gently to and fro. Bedroom windows opened and lace curtains and the melody of vacuums unfurled.

My heart began to beat faster and louder than before. I felt like a hero, a first traveller in an unknown land.

If I'd wanted to, I could have leapt from that pavement and walked upon the peaceful air. But I didn't because later, I saw the mirrored garden and went in.

I had dawdled through the shabby high street, which smelt of vinegar from the chippies and old, unwashed clothes. Mum would have adored it: there were charity shops from end to end. I glanced at this and that, then drifted down towards the sea.

I leant over the railings and stared at families on the beach. Their white shoulders were going red, their plastic seaside stuff was piled around on the sand. No sign of Dad's sculptures, but I saw his donkeys, waiting in a row. If I hadn't had the sandwiches in my hand, I'd have asked how much, and climbed up.

I wandered along the promenade, biting into the warm, fishy bread and then the jam. As I tipped back my head and put Gran's bottle of squash to my lips, I saw something flash, and for once I didn't turn away. I walked across.

The mirrored garden was in the space between a pink bungalow and the last terraced house. Two children with sandy legs, stood on the pavement and stared.

'Come *on*,' their mother, or somebody like one, nagged. 'You don't want to look at *that*!' But they did so she grabbed their hands, and dragged them past.

I drained the bottle and went in.

There were no flowers in the garden or anything that grew with roots and stems and fluttering green leaves. Instead, someone had gathered up the remains of all the broken and shattered things in the world: ends of green wine bottles, triangles of blue willow pattern with pagodas and stick-like trees; pebbles and shells and thick fragments of pottery soaked in an old, yellow glaze. Someone had collected these thousands and thousands of smashed and abandoned bits together and cemented them into place. Then they'd built towers and spires and houses the size of shoe boxes and paths and a mountain with tea-cup white peaks of snow above a turquoise tiled sea. Everywhere, mirrors and bits of mirrors had been set into the concrete and they sparkled and flashed and blazed.

It was ugly and beautiful and it must have taken someone years and years.

'Oh, it did,' said a voice at my elbow as if I had spoken aloud. 'Twenty-eight, to be exact. And I'm not finished yet.'

I nodded. I understood what he meant.

'Like it, do you?' He was a small, sun-burnt man with a thin mouth and wild, wiry hair.

I nodded again. In a cracked mirror I saw myself fractured into a million pieces of light, and scattered around.

The man's nails were broken, his hands ugly and worn. I imagined him walking with shoulders bent and eyes downcast. His pockets would bulge as he scoured the ground.

I don't know how long I spent in the mirrored garden, but I had to run through the summer shadows to make it back in time.

'Had a nice day, dear?' Gran helped me to more chips.

'Yes.'

'Your father phoned.'

'What did he say?' I could barely get my breath.

'Not much. The weather was hot.'

'You'd expect that,' Grandpa speared a pea, 'in Spain.'

That night I left the flowered curtains open and imagined things in the moonlight as I lay on the narrow bed.

'See that?' The next afternoon the man pointed to a circle of mirrored petals around half a plastic throne. 'That's where I started, twenty-eight years ago.'

'Oh.' I hadn't asked but it was nice to know. I scratched the skin on the back of my knee. Earlier, I'd ridden a donkey up and down the beach and now I itched. 'It's very...' I stared at the little drops of reflected light which danced on a doll's hand, and a piece of smoothed, bleached bone.

'Isn't it just.' He sighed and set something straight. 'But now I don't really care.'

'Don't you?'

'No. Or not much. Or I say something back. But mainly I just keep quiet and do a bit more. Like over there. See? That's where I'm working now.'

'What'll you do when it's finished?'

'Finished?' He rubbed his hands together and his rough skin rustled like leaves. 'It'll never be that.'

Back at the house after supper, I dried while Grandpa washed up. 'A mirrored garden?' He paused as he steered the head of the mop round the rim of a glass. 'On the *promenade*, did you say, Chris? I don't think I've heard about that.' He looked down at Jasper. 'But we don't go far now, do we, old boy?'

The dog didn't move.

'But it's been there twenty-eight years! That's what the man said.'

'Has it really? Just think of that.' Grandpa rinsed out the bowl and squeezed the mop.

That night I heard a summer storm in my dreams and when I woke in the morning, everything smelled wet. Before I left, I held up the basin of wrung-out clothes while Gran pegged out the wash. Later, I walked barefooted on the cold, ridged sand. I ate my sandwiches and spent time with a little kid who was trying to fish off the rocks.

I heard the noise as I was walking back. It was like thunder with a car crash thrown in. When I'd belted up the littered, sandy steps I saw a cloud of dust that was as dark as smoke. A small, sunburnt workman had stopped the traffic and held back the curious crowd as the bulldozers moved in.

'What are they doing?' I cried out to no one in particular, so no one answered back.

In ten minutes the mirrored garden had gone and the place where it had been was flat. The workman stepped back, and the seaside traffic moved once more. The holiday crowd licked ice cream and rolled on. The workman connected up the water and began to hose down the billowing dust. As I watched, he bent down and picked up something that flashed. He rubbed it clean with his hand, then put it carefully in the pocket of his jeans.

'Your father phoned,' Gran was pouring custard into Jasper's bowl. 'They'll be back tomorrow, like they said.' She smiled as she tipped the rest into a jug.

I smiled as I watched Jasper lap.

And I was glad, really. I was glad.

**Lesley Howarth**

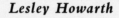

mirrors dot com

*Illustration by Tim Stevens*

## *Lesley Howarth*

## mirrors dot com

It started four days before Samantha Lamb's birthday.

You know there's a Year of the Rat, a Year of the Pig, the Dog, the Horse, in the Chinese calendar? They knew more than we did, the people who started that stuff.

I know about that stuff now. Did you know there's an animal – a secret self – hidden in your reflection? Oh, yes. And the way to see it is—

But I'd better start at the beginning.

My friend Sam's birthday was coming up, so I searched the Internet for these mirrors. Sam likes stuff for her room, and I knew she'd just broken one. Finally I found a site selling mirrors. It took an age to download the graphics. But when they popped up, I was gobsmacked.

They were pretty amazing mirrors. Twisted spirals of silver around shapes that looked like wolves' heads. Mirrors like the shields of knights in battle. Gilt 'chimney glasses' crested with eagles. Copies of Roman hand-mirrors shaped like the sun. Unbreakable mirrors of polished metal. Used by explorers, the site said. And all at pub/mirror.com. I didn't know mirrors like that existed. I'd never seen anything like them.

I actually never meant to order it.

Those mirrors – especially the glaring wolf's head with the burning ruby eyes – seemed to jump out at me, to *make* me click on them and order them. I'll never know why I put the wolf-mirror into my 'shopping trolley'. Next thing, I'd OKd Mum's credit card number and the wolf man was on his way.

He actually turned up in the cat flap next day. The postman pops parcels through the cat flap whenever there's no one at home. When I saw the package labelled PUB/MIRROR WORLDWIDE in the darkness of the garage, I felt very slightly sick. As though his burning ruby eyes could read my mind through the bubble-wrap already, and he knew that he wasn't wanted.

'And where are you going to put *that*?' Mum's reflection looked back at her disgustedly from the silvery depths of the wolf-mirror.

'I'm not. It's for Sam's birthday.'

'Good job. He gives me the creeps.'

He gave me the creeps, too, actually.

The wolf man curling around the mirror glared down at me before I went to school. His grinning face, resting on the top of the mirror and hanging down over the edge of it, glared down at me when I came home. His silver paws hugged the sides of it and glinted in the moonlight that leaked in at night around the sides of my blind, and felt like they'd like to hug me too, and not in a friendly way. I got up and put him outside.

I forgot about him until I fell over him on my way to the bathroom next morning. He toppled over on to my feet and lay looking up at me, still creeping around his mirror like some twisted mythical beast.

*I don't even like you. Get off me*!

Three days until Sam's birthday.

Why didn't I send him back?

You know in fairy stories, there's always a forbidden thing, something the person in the story mustn't do, and then they always go and do it? DON'T forget to go home at midnight. DON'T go into the woods alone. DON'T forget to drop the enchanted nut into the sea for your magic griffin to rest on, all that stuff? I began to wonder about the mirror man, the more his ruby eyes got to me. What did he do, to be stuck there like that, hugging his mirror and hoping someone might want him over the Net?

'Did you get me something?' Sam asked.

'Something?'

'A birthday present?'

'Oh, yeah,' I said. 'I got you a present. I got you a present, all right.'

I tried to send him back that night, but Returns weren't optioned at all, and pub/mirror.com came up with some boring looking pub mirrors, as if that was what they were selling. 'What happened to the wolf-mirror?' I mailed them.

'Gothic Series Sold Out', was the only reply. No Returns even mentioned, not even a PO Box to send them to.

I was stuck with him, and I knew it. Two more days, then Sam would have to have him in *her* bedroom. Some birthday present. I knew, even then, I should bury him under the noodles and cans in the dustbin and buy Samantha Lamb something else.

But by that time it was too late.

It had come to me as I was lying in bed waiting to go to sleep. I'd just seen ER and my mind wouldn't stop. You know the feeling. Not good. The moonlight always came in around the side of my blind, and that night it silvered the claws of the wolf-mirror and made a pale glow in its depths.

I got up and turned him to face the wall.

Then I got back into bed.

I could feel the power in his red-eyed glare, even with his back to the room. The moonlight flooded in anyway, and suddenly I knew what the forbidden thing was, as certainly as if it had been chalked on the back of the mirror, where his silver claws appeared around the backing.

*Don't look into the mirror by moonlight, or you'll see what animal you are.*

I sat up in bed. What *animal* you are?

I got up and moved the mirror, very carefully, out of my room.

'What on earth are you doing?' Dad wondered, coming up the stairs to bed.

'I don't like him in my room at night,' I told him sheepishly.

'I'm not surprised, it's hideous. I thought it had four legs.'

'It has.' I checked him. 'There's one at the back.'

'Night, then,' Dad said.

'Night, night.'

Sweet dreams, I almost added, except I didn't get any, myself. Instead, I had the moonlight leaking in around the blind and the feeling that grew and kept me awake until it was driving me mad.

Two feelings, actually.

One was the certainty that if I got up to go to the loo and had to walk past the wolf-man I wouldn't be able to stop myself *looking into the mirror by moonlight.*

The other was the certainty that he'd had all four legs

wrapped around the front of the mirror, and no leg down the back.

In the end I had to get up.

I made it past the mirror to the toilet, though his ruby eyes scorched my ankles. I made it back as far as the bedroom door before I let myself see, through half-closed eyes, the place where the wolf-man had been.

His mirror glared down the stair-well, reflecting the outside light that leaked up the stairs in the darkness; a plain, silver-edged mirror, so ordinary you might even have ordered it from pub/mirror.com, or from any shop selling candles, or any department store.

The wolf-man was gone, I didn't like to think where.

I must have knocked him off his perch in passing; probably he'd rolled down the stairs. Probably if I looked I'd see him, forlorn and glinting, in the hall.

But I didn't look.

Instead I slept on the landing in the sleeping bag I found in the airing cupboard, too scared to go into my room.

In the early hours, a flash of silver seemed to tumble into my dreams. The glare of ruby eyes reminded me, over and over again, of the *one thing I knew I mustn't do.*

Dad fell over me at seven o'clock.

'Lisa! What on earth—?'

I turned over. 'Dad.'

A hammering headache filled the whole of my brain. Those burning eyes had drilled into the back of my head. They saw what I really was, reflected in their own fiery depths.

'Where's that—'

'Mirror?' Dad set it straight. 'Must have fallen over in the night.'

There he was, but he didn't fool me.

So the mirror-man was back on his mirror, with his wolf-legs folded around it as if he'd never been gone. Flashing around like a slip of silver all night. He'd changed his position, anyone could see. What did he think, we were stupid?

'Why aren't you in your bed?' Dad bleated.

'Doesn't matter, does it?' I said, turning over. 'Leave me alone,' I growled.

The next night was Friday night, and we went to the cinema for Sam's birthday treat, as her party was going to be only *part* of her birthday, as Sam gets everything she wants. The film was OK, not great. We spilled a whole tub of popcorn over the floor, plus these stupid boys kept annoying us, but anyway, it was all right.

When I got home I remembered him. The mirror-man upstairs. I delayed for as long as I could. But finally I had to go to bed.

It was the worst night yet. I finally got off to sleep all right, which I don't usually after a Jumbo Cola and a giant bag of Pik 'n' Mix, which was pants, as they had the wrong prawns and massively big worms, so you have to pay five quid to get *one*.

So at last I was just drifting off. I don't know, I may have been asleep – when I thought I saw him running round my room. Quick as quicksilver, the mirror-man, wolfing my slippers and flashing over my desk, his red eyes burning, his tongue slavering, his quick tail flicking and whipping.

Who was he? The reflection of someone's secret self, the last person to look into that mirror in the moonlight, after they'd ordered it by mistake? That mirror, that mirror, that mirror. Had been the cause of it.

I started up in fright and launched myself at that mirror.

In the moment before I smashed it, I saw what animal I

was. The wolf rolled off the top of it and raged and boiled on the carpet, *changing shape as I watched into the animal that was me*, until I put my pillow on top of it, and another pillow on top of that, and my dressing gown and a pile of books, and everything I could find to weigh it down and stop it, that reflection of my secret self…

'Happy birthday!' Sam wishes herself, her head around Lisa's bedroom door on Saturday morning. 'I let myself in, all right?'

Sam waits, but nothing happens; no move to get her her present. Instead, Lisa puzzles over the pieces of a mirror. Not a very nice mirror, either.

'What are you doing?'

'What does it look like? I just have to piece it together. Then I can send it back.'

Sam picks up a twist of silver. 'What's this?'

'What does it look like?'

'A dragon?'

'It *was* a wolf, but the wolf-man's gone.'

Sam looks at the dragon's curved limbs, at the shape it's designed to hold, its tail licking clean round an oval. 'What's this meant to be for?'

'He sits on top of the mirror,' Lisa supplies. 'When he's not—'

'What?'

'Broken,'

'You said, alive.'

Lisa's eyes flash. 'I said, broken.'

Sam looks at her friend. 'About my party tonight—'

'Mind if I take it back?' Lisa scratches Sam very slightly as she reached up to grab the figure. Blood wells up on Sam's hand, in a ruby-red spot on her thumb. Lisa watches her eyes, and Sam gets the strangest feeling she's looking into the mouth of a—

The dragon in Lisa's eyes smiles. 'Thanks.' Her fingernails close over the silver figure and place it over the top of the mirror-puzzle.

'It's my birthday.' Sam sucks the scratch on her hand. 'This isn't supposed to happen.'

But Lisa has eyes for no one but herself, mirrored in the scattered pieces of glass that make up a jigsaw on the floor. 'Ever look into a mirror at night? After I mend it, you can put this in your room and see what animal *you* are.'

Sam Lamb knows already. She leaves the bedroom, unnoticed, as downstairs Dad logs on to the computer and finds pub/mirrors.com offering 'Reduced Gothic Mirrors at a Fraction of their Former Price', over the search he makes for a book.

'Lisa! That dot com company's got those mirrors again!' Dad yells up the stairs as a range of extraordinary mirrors appear when he clicks on them without meaning to. 'Like that weird mirror you just got!'

His voice washes over Lisa, guarding her broken mirror upstairs, seeing her fragmented face in it.

*Me and not me. Who am I?*

*For a moment, I can see a reflection of myself as I might be. The girl in the mirror is me. Me, and not me, at the same time. I'm not sure I wanted to know, but I did what I knew I shouldn't…*

*I can hear Dad downstairs, ordering a mirror. I want to stop him, but I can't. He will release his inner self. What animal will he be? A pig, a rat, a rabbit?*

Dad's voice comes up the stairs. 'You know, these mirrors aren't bad – 'Gothic Mirror in Gilt' – I think I might – oh, I *have* clicked on it, what a stupid donkey I am, I think I might have just ordered it…'

*Jeremy Strong*

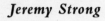

NEVER TRUST A PARROT

*Illustration by Tim Stevens*

## Jeremy Strong

### NEVER TRUST A PARROT

*Dear Pet Problem Page,*
*You are my last chance of hope. I pray that you can help me. I*
*have a problem with my parrot. I had better start at the*
*beginning – there is so much that needs explaining...*

Jamie had never actually met a parrot that could talk
before, but this parrot could not only talk but it had a

lisp and couldn't say its 'r's properly. 'I am your fwend,' it said, and fixed Jamie with a beady eye. Jamie gazed back into the black obsidian-like eye, almost hypnotised.

'I like you too,' he replied.

The parrot walked up the inside of its cage, the way parrots do, and hung from the roof. It stared at Jamie with its other eye, clicked its tongue, stretched its wings and then said, 'My name is Nemethith.'

'Nemesis,' repeated Jamie.

The parrot began screeching furiously, clattering its wings against the bars of the cage. 'Nemethith!' squawked the enraged bird. 'Nemethith!'

'Keep your feathers on,' muttered Jamie crossly.

The parrot lunged forward, grabbing one of Jamie's fingers in its beak.

'Ow! Let go, you monster!'

'I am your fwend,' hissed Nemesis through his clenched beak.

'No you're not. Let go!' At last Jamie managed to wrench his hand away from the cage. He examined his finger. There were two purple welts, clear marks of the parrot's powerful beak. Jamie shook his hand in pain and rubbed the finger. At least there was no blood. He shot an angry glance at the bird. Parrots cannot smile, but Nemesis was doing a pretty good impression. Maybe it was the peculiar shape of the beak. Both the upper and lower mandibles had a single raised point on each side. Strange, thought Jamie.

*At first I thought it would be fun to have a pet parrot, especially one that could talk. Nemesis is a South American Paradise Parrot. He bit me on the very first day I got him. He bit Mum and Dad too. I suppose I should have started worrying at that point, but how was I to know that horror was just around the corner? If it hadn't been for that little mirror I might never have known, but I'd better fill in a bit more detail first...*

The parrot had come from Jamie's aunt, who had seen him in a pet shop. Aunt Cleo was immediately seduced by the parrot's fabulous colouring, the black glitter of his eyes and the wonderful way in which he greeted Cleo's entrance into the shop. 'Hail to Her Majethty, Empweth of the Fowetht!'

Aunt Cleo bought the parrot on the spot, despite the fact that she was always going away on business and so couldn't be around to look after it much. She gave it to Jamie's family to care for instead. Aunt Cleo was like that. She was always buying animals and then giving them to Jamie's family. So far they had a giant lop-eared rabbit (*Cleo: 'It's got ears like blankets!'*), a chameleon (*Cleo: You'll never have another fly in the house!*), a llama they kept in the garden (*Cleo: A llama is the best burglar deterrent you can have, in fact it's a burglar allarma!*), and now a parrot.

But Nemesis was different. For a start he could speak, and then there were those dark eyes, as dark as the depths of a tropical rain forest by night; a darkness haunted by the soft footfall of the passing jaguar, and the silent slither of the anaconda. There was something of the night in Nemesis, especially the way he skulked in his cage, cracking open sunflower seeds and spitting the shells at Jamie while he slept. Then he'd whisper, 'I am your fwend.'

Jamie tried to teach Nemesis some *new* words. In revenge for the bite on his finger Jamie began with, 'Around the ragged rocks the ragged rascal ran.' This of course came out as, 'Awound the wagged wocks,' which was as far as Nemesis got, before clicking his tongue in disapproval and hanging upside down. Jamie had already learnt that this was usually a warning that the bird was about to have a temper tantrum. Sometimes the parrot seemed more human than bird.

Three days after the arrival of Nemesis, Jamie felt his injured finger itching and scratched it. That was when he first noticed the tiny fluff that had gathered round the edge of the bruising. He showed it to his mother.

'When your skin itches like that, it's a good sign. It shows that the cut is healing,' she said.

'My finger wasn't cut. It was just sort of – squeezed, very hard,' Jamie pointed out. 'By a parrot.'

His mother smiled brightly. 'I'm sure it's on the mend,' she insisted, and clicked her tongue, as if to underline everything.

*It was not long after Nemesis bit me that other things began to happen.*

*The apple tree in the garden suddenly put on a growing spurt. It was early summer and I put it down to all the rain we'd been having, but then the leaves began to enlarge. They fattened and lengthened and grew darker and denser. Day by day we watched the apple tree grow until it was three times the size of our other trees. It dwarfed everything around it. Mum and Dad thought it was wonderful, but I thought it was weird, and then Dad actually climbed it until he was sitting amongst the high branches. I was just boggling at this when Mum suddenly whizzed up the tree and joined him.*

*As for Nemesis, he spent all his time staring out through the bars of his cage. He would make little clucking noises and sometimes let out a long, growly sigh. I thought that maybe he was bored...*

One day Jamie was passing a pet shop and on a sudden impulse he went in. He wondered what little toys he might take home for the parrot to play with. Nemesis must be getting pretty fed up, shut in a cage most of the time. Jamie bought a bell and a mirror. They were really meant for budgerigars but, as the pet shop man said, parrots are just very big budgies really.

Nemesis hated the bell. He pulled it right off its little chain and cast it out through the bars of the cage. It rolled away under the sofa, where it stayed. So that was the end of that.

As for the mirror, that was where the trouble began. If it hadn't been for the mirror, Jamie might never have known, never begun to wonder. Jamie was not sure whether to bless or curse the mirror, but there was no doubting its effect.

Nemesis did not seem at all bothered by the mirror. What Jamie noticed was this: when Nemesis looked in the mirror he didn't see a parrot looking back at him. He didn't see anything at all. *Nemesis didn't have a reflection.*

At first Jamie assumed that the mirror was no good, and he went storming back to the pet shop. 'This mirror is defunct,' he said. 'It's not a mirror. It's a piece of glass.' But the pet shop man looked in it and saw himself, and when Jamie took the trouble of peering in, he was there too.

Jamie, who by this time was not only puzzled but worried, returned home, took the parrot into the bathroom and held him up in front of the big mirror above the wash basin. Jamie was there, holding up his arm, but there was no parrot. Jamie paled. He knew there was only one creature that had no reflection in a mirror, and that was a *vampire*.

As for Nemesis himself, he turned away from the mirror and gazed at Jamie with his eyes that were now like black holes in the fabric of space. 'I am your fwend,' he said, quietly.

Jamie was faced with the unpleasant observation that he was harbouring a vampire parrot – a vampire parrot with a speech impediment. Then he remembered his finger.

*It was when I noticed the tiny feathers on my finger that I became seriously concerned. The fluff that had first appeared around my bruise had now turned to feathers. Of course they were very small, but they were also unmistakeable. I couldn't show Mum and Dad because I have hardly seen them since yesterday. I had to make my own lunch and supper. They seem to spend all their time up in the trees that have taken over our garden. The trees sprang up overnight, a miniature rain forest. Some of them are laden with exotic fruits that are eaten by the troops of monkeys that race along the highest branches, crashing amongst the dense leaves.*

*As for Nemesis, I swear he is now grinning at me. When I went to sleep last night, I dreamed that he was talking to me in a really sweet, kind voice, so smooth and soft. I would wake, sweating, but he was always fast asleep in his cage...*

Outside the house, monkeys whooped and howled. Great birds sang and burbled amongst the dark branches, and occasionally a glimpse of yellow and black signalled the stealthy passing of the jaguar.

At night the parrot's eyes would snap open and Nemesis would stare across at Jamie as he slept. Then the parrot would begin his night whispers, in a soft, crooning voice. 'Thoon you will be mine. Together we thall wule the world. Thoon you will be a pawott like your pawenth. There ith no ethcape, for I am Nature'th methenger and it ith time for her to weclaim the world. Humanth have methed it up and now jungle thall cover the earth and all the wagged wocks wunth more and there will be no humanth at all. Ha ha ha ha.'

Jamie saw his parents one more time. They were sitting together on the branch of a tree at the edge of the spreading forest. Their clothes had gone, and their bodies were covered in glowing feathers. Dad cocked his head on one side and gazed at Jamie, as if he were trying to remember who he was. They made their way down from the tree and stepped on to what was left of the lawn, but they wouldn't come any closer.

'Mum? Dad?' Jamie didn't know what to say.

His mother lifted one arm, as if she was inviting Jamie to join them. She clicked her tongue several times. Jamie's father opened his mouth and cawed. The hair on his head suddenly rose up in a crest and he cawed again. Then they went back into the forest. Jamie returned to the house on his own. He wandered into the kitchen and opened another packet of sunflower seeds. He began cracking them and spitting out the shells. They crunched beneath his feet: thousands of them, in every room.

*I try not to listen to Nemesis but it is becoming more and more difficult. Part of the problem is that I am now covered from head to foot with feathers. I can no longer wear clothes. Every now and then I get this uncontrollable urge to stand on the arm of the sofa, furiously flapping my arms, wanting to jump. I keep trying to walk up walls and hang from the light fittings.*

*I have tried all the usual vampire remedies but they don't seem to work on parrots. Nemesis seems to be invincible and every hour I become more like him.*

*What am I to do? The jungle has spread right the way down our street and across the park. I haven't seen another human for days.*

*Please help. You are my last hope. I cannot write any longer. It is too difficult to grip the pen with my thin claws. I am desperate. I looked in the mirror this morning and I wasn't there. Who am I? What am I? What is going to happen to me? I am your fwend. I am your fwend. I am…*

*Malorie Blackman*

Watching

*Illustration by Tim Stevens*

## *Malorie Blackman*

### WATCHING

Have you ever wanted something so badly, so completely that it doesn't just become part of you, you become part of it? Have you ever longed for something so much that you can't think of anything else, can't feel for anything else? Everything else just fades away into nothingness. Well, that's the way it is with me and acting. I mean it. I want to act. I'm no good at anything else because I've never really concentrated on anything else. From the time I was seven or eight, whenever anyone asked me what I wanted to be when I grew up, the answer was always the same. An actress. At first my family thought it was sweet. Now they don't. I don't think the woman in the mirror likes it either.

But she doesn't scare me any more. Well, hardly ever. Most of the time she just sits there, staring at me. Sometimes she speaks... but I can't hear a word she's saying. Her lips move either very slowly or in a frantic rush, like a face on a TV screen when someone's messing about with the fast-forward or slow-mo buttons. She talks and talks at me – but I can't hear a word. I just shake my head at her now, or turn away. I can't understand what she's trying to tell me and, to be honest, I don't think I want to. I stopped trying to listen a long time ago. Sometimes tears trickle down her cheeks. Silent tears. But I don't mind any more. I'm used to her now. It took a while, I must admit. I mean, the first time I saw her, I screamed blue murder. One moment I was sitting there in front of my dressing table, combing my hair and minding my own business, when an unexpected tangle sent the comb flicking out of my hand. I bent down to pick it up and when I straightened up, *she* was there – in the mirror – staring straight back at me. I shrieked and turned. There was no one behind me. I turned back to the mirror. The old woman was still there, staring. That's when I lost it. I mean, you'd have to have nerves made of diamond not to scream at something like that. I leapt up and ran for my bedroom door.

Mum and Dad came charging up the stairs and into my bedroom.

'What is it? What's the matter?'

I swung around to point at my mirror. 'There's someone in my room.'

'What?' Dad immediately started searching around, hopping about like a demented kangaroo. 'There's someone in your room? Where? What did he look like? Josie, call the police!'

I grabbed Mum's arm as she headed out the door to do as Dad had asked. 'Mum, it wasn't a man, it was a woman. An old woman. And she wasn't in my room. I mean, she was but she wasn't.'

'Alexa, you're not making any sense,' Mum frowned.

'She never does!' said my younger sister, Jackie.

I took a deep breath the way I always did whenever Jackie opened her mouth, and tried again. 'Mum, I looked in my mirror and there was an old woman staring back at me.'

Mum and Dad exchanged a sceptical, 'is-our-child-losing-her-marbles?' look.

'I'm not making it up and I'm not crazy,' I shouted.

'Maybe you dozed off…' Dad began.

'I didn't do that either.' I marched to the mirror. 'I'm telling you there was an old woman in there, looking at me.'

Jackie came further into the room to stand next to me. She pointed at the mirror.

'Well, there's only my gorgeous reflection and your scabby one in there now,' she said.

Mum and Dad and Jackie all started laughing – which just infuriated me even more.

'Get lost, Jackie.' I hissed at her. 'You know you're not allowed in my room.'

'Your sister was just teasing,' Dad smiled.

'I don't care. I hate her! She's always following me around and poking and prying into my things.'

'Don't take it out on me, just 'cause you're cracking up,' Jackie sniffed.

'Out! Get out of my room – NOW!'

'Won't.'

I took a step forward. Jackie turned and ran – which was very wise of her.

'That wasn't very nice,' said Mum.

'That's right, take her side the way you always do,' I scorned. 'She's not allowed in here. My room is a little-kid free zone. And you two can leave now as well.'

'Now wait just a minute…' Dad started.

Mum touched his arm and shook her head. They both left my room without saying another word. Dad was mad as hell at me – as usual. Mum was desperately trying to keep the peace – as usual. And I couldn't care less, as usual. I heard Dad muttering about 'teenagers' as he went downstairs.

That's what happened the first time I saw the old woman in my mirror. That was almost a year ago. Hard to believe, a whole year has gone by. Mum and Dad just shout at me these days. We don't talk any more. We quarrel – vicious and sarcastic. Every word that doesn't erupt in a shout leads up to, or follows behind the nasty, bitter things we say to each other. Jackie and I barely talk to each other now. She finally got the message that I can't stand her, so now she can't stand me. Mum and Dad call me a typical teenager. I don't want to be a typical anything. And as for the old woman in the mirror, I see her far more frequently these days, but like I said, she doesn't bother me any more.

I can't wait until I am old enough to leave home. I have my whole life mapped out. I'm going to be an actress. Not one of those work-for-two-weeks-of-the-year actresses. No, thank you very much. I'm going to be successful. I'm going to be *famous*. I'm going to be a STAR. I'm going to feature in TV programmes and films which millions and millions of people will watch. You just wait and see if I don't. And no one's going to get in my way. Not Dad and Mum. Not my sister, Jackie. Not even the old woman in the mirror. No one.

She waited for her sister to pick up the phone. The moment she heard her sister's voice, she launched in.

'Hi, Jackie. How are you?'

'Oh, hello Alexa…'

She tried to ignore the cool, unwelcoming tone of her

sister's voice. 'It's good to hear you. How's Julian? And my nephews?'

'Fine…'

'Wasn't it your wedding anniversary last month?'

'That's right.'

She'd heard that Jackie and Julian had splashed out on a huge wedding-anniversary party. She hadn't been invited.

'Thirty-five years… That's a long time to be married.'

'Yes, it is,' her sister agreed politely.

Silence.

'I… I was just wondering if you'd all like to spend Christmas with me.'

'I don't think that's a…'

'Oh, come on, Jackie. I've got a great big house going begging.' She rushed on before her sister could cast her usual rejection in her direction. 'It'd be great to see you and my nephews and their kids. You'd all be welcome.'

'We've made different plans,' Jackie said. 'My sons and their families are coming over to me for Christmas. It's all arranged.'

'I'd be more than happy to have you all visit me here.'

'I don't think so, Alexa,' Jackie said quietly.

Silence. Silence that stretched through the time and space and years between them.

'Then maybe...' She swallowed hard, forcing herself to continue. 'Maybe, I could come to your house for Christmas?'

'I don't think that's a good idea either.'

'Why not?'

'Alexa,' Jackie made no attempt to hide her exasperation. 'We haven't spoken in almost forty years and now suddenly you're always on the phone asking about my family. What's that about? When you became rich and famous you told all kinds of lies about me and Mum and Dad. You even said you were an only child. How d'you think that made me feel?'

'That was a long time ago, Jackie. I didn't know any better then.'

'Well, you should've done,' her sister shot back. 'You turned your back on all of us years ago. Are we meant to start cheering because you now deign to have us back in your life?'

'I guess not.'

'You didn't even come to Dad's funeral,' Jackie accused.

'I've already explained…'

'Yeah, I know. Another premiere, or filming to be done or a theatre audience to wow, or a party to go to, or an appointment to have your nails polished that you just couldn't get out of.'

'That's not fair. It wasn't like that.'

'It was from where Mum and I were standing.'

'Which still didn't give you the right not to tell me about Mum's funeral.' She couldn't mask her bitterness.

'Alexa, if you couldn't give a damn about Mum when she was alive, why on earth would you care about her when she died?'

'I did care…'

'You phoned her twice a year – on her birthday and at Christmas.'

'I tried…'

'Look, I'm not going through all this again,' Jackie interrupted. 'I think… I think it'd be better if you didn't phone me again.'

'But Jackie please…'

'I mean it, Alexa. You've made your choices in life and we were never included. I'm not going to allow my family to be your latest hobby, so leave us alone.'

The phone clicked as her sister put down the receiver. Slowly, she replaced hers too. She stared at herself in her dressing-table mirror. Here she was, an old woman who looked even older than her years and what did she have to show for her life? A couple of tarnished acting awards in a gilt and glass fronted cabinet. She had a big house which she hated, because she was like a ghost in it. Days spent talking to herself in the mirrors around the house, just so she'd have someone to talk to. Oh, she had someone to cook and clean for her, but that was all. Three ex-husbands and no children later, she had nothing to show for her life. For all the good she'd done in this world, it wouldn't've made any difference if she hadn't been born at all. She knew she was feeling sorry for herself, being sad and pathetic – but it was the truth. And the worst thing was, her life was all her own doing. She'd run after packaging and thrown away the content. If only she could warn the girl she used to be. If only she could get through to her. If only... Sometimes she could feel her life, her very soul slipping into the mirror before her. It was the only thing left from her childhood, the only thing she'd kept. These days she just sat and stared at it, losing herself in it.

Until the girl appeared. There she was now. At last. In the mirror. Alexa used to think it must be her mind playing tricks on her. Her mind played tricks on her a lot these days. There the girl was, watching in the mirror. Watching. And shaking her head. And frowning. Alexa had to get through to her. There must be a way to get through to her. She couldn't give up. She wouldn't. Her past was at stake.

'Alexa, can I come in?' Jackie popped her head around my door.

'No, you can't. Go away.'

Jackie came into my bedroom anyway. I turned in my chair to glare at her. 'Am I talking Martian? Get lost!'

'Alexa,' Jackie hovered uncertainly. 'Why... why don't you like me?'

I opened my mouth to let rip. Only something about Jackie stopped me from saying a word. It was the look on her face, or maybe the unhappy, slouchy way she was standing. She was actually upset. More than upset — unhappy. I took a deep breath.

'Jackie, it's not you. It's this place, Mum and Dad. Me.' I sighed. 'I want to get up and get out so badly I can almost… almost touch it sometimes.'

I reached out my hands towards the mirror which showed only my reflection now.

'Why d'you want to be an actress so much?'

' 'Cause it's the only thing I'm good at. Because I can close my eyes and when I open them again, I can be anyone or anything I want to be. And people watch me. They watch *me.*' I closed my eyes, willing the years away, willing myself to be older, so much older. 'D'you have any idea how that feels?'

'No…' Jackie replied.

I'd almost forgotten my sister was in the room. I turned towards her again. 'No, I don't suppose you do.' I wasn't trying to be snide — for once. But in that one moment, I realised how different Jackie and I were. 'What d'you want to be when you're older?'

She looked surprised. I couldn't blame her. This was the longest conversation we'd had in months.

'I don't know. Maybe a teacher, or a taxi driver.'

I laughed. I couldn't help it. 'You're so young! You're nine going on nineteen months!'

'And you're fourteen going on forty. Mum says you're in too much of a hurry to grow up.'

'You don't understand. No one understands,' I turned away from Jackie, shaking my head.

'Explain it to me then,' Jackie said.

'I... I can't. It's something you either get or you don't. Just go away, okay?'

I waited for the sound of the door to close. It wasn't long coming. I turned to make sure my sister really had left the room. No one understood. Dad had had the same job for over twenty years. Every night he came home and complained about it but he had no choice. He had to go back to the same job each day. And Mum did a bit of temping whenever money was short – which was most of the time. A bit of typing here, a receptionist there. A cashier here, a waitress there. I didn't want to do that. There had to be more to life than that, but if I got too close to Mum and Dad and even Jackie, they'd keep me in their world. I didn't want to stay in their world. I wanted something different. I wanted something more. And I was going to get it too.

She could've had children. Her first two husbands had tried to persuade her to have children. But she'd said no. They would've got in the way of her career. No one wanted to film a pregnant body, at least that was what she told her husbands. The timing wasn't right. Her latest contract wouldn't allow it. The moon wasn't bright enough or big enough or close enough to Earth. Any and every excuse. And for what?

Old reviews crept into her head, every word memorised. Every word burned into her.

*'Alexa Langland makes the mistake of believing that all she has to do is look good, for the audience to forgive her complete lack of acting ability.'*

*'Alexa Langland acts with the depth and emotion of a soggy tissue. It makes you wonder if she's ever experienced a real, selfless emotion in her life. To judge by her acting, this critic for one, seriously doubts it.'*

And so on. And so forth. And whilst her looks lasted, so did the job offers. But they'd both disappeared a long time ago.

She looked at herself in the mirror again, hating what she saw but unable to tear her gaze away. She dabbed some more foundation powder on to her powder puff and applied it to her skin, then rubbed it in. It wasn't working. Nothing was working. It was too late for her. But somehow, she would make the girl she used to be understand. Before it was too late. She picked up the puff and rubbed it furiously all over the mirror. She didn't want to see herself.

But she did want to see herself – as she was. She stood up slowly, using the sleeve of her silk dress to rub the powder off the mirror. Her face looked distorted now, partially hidden behind swirls of make-up. She wiped harder. If she could just make the girl listen. Listen. Listen. Before it was too late.


I turned back to the mirror. She made me jump! There she is again – that old woman, staring at me from inside the mirror. I'm not the least bit scared of her. She just gets on my last nerve now, that's all. She always stares at me with that sad look on her face. When I'm a famous actress and stinking rich, I won't ever let myself get that old. Ah, she's shaking her head at me. The old woman in the mirror is frowning at me. Why is she always frowning? Maybe she can read my mind? I don't care. I'm going to be famous. You just see if I don't. And no one will stand in my way. Not my mum and dad. Not my sister, Jackie. Not even that stupid woman in the mirror, watching me. Watching me. Watching.

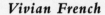

*Vivian French*

SELIM-HASSAN THE SEVENTH

*Illustration by Tim Stevens*

## Vivian French

### SELIM-HASSAN THE SEVENTH

Selim-Hassan the Seventh lived in Pushnapanjipetal, which is and was famous for nothing at all, except for the extreme hairiness of all the men who lived there. Selim-Hassan's father was the village barber. Every day he soaped and lathered and foamed the beards of the men of the village and then, with eight swift swoops of his shining silver razor, shaved them so smoothly that their skin felt like the softest silk.

'Look in the mirror!' Selim-Hassan's father would say. And the customer would peer at himself in Selim-Hassan's splendid gilt-edged mirror decorated with golden roses, and nod.

'You are right, Selim-Hassan the Sixth. It is indeed the finest shave that I have ever had.'

Selim-Hassan's grandfather had been a barber. So also had his great-grandfather, his great-great-grandfather, and his great-great-great-grandfather. Each of them in turn had practised and refined the art of shaving from twelve swift swoops of the shining silver razor to eleven, from eleven to ten, from ten to nine. Each of them in turn had passed on their skills and knowledge to their grateful oldest son.

Selim-Hassan the Seventh was different. He did *not* want to be a barber. He was not in the least grateful when his father showed him how to sharpen the razors on a wetted stone. He was not at all grateful when he was given the opportunity to sweep up the curls and whiskers on the shop floor. He was positively rude when a customer asked him to pass him a hot towel.

Selim-Hassan's father grew anxious. 'Could it be,' he

asked Selim-Hassan's mother, 'that our son takes after his great-great-great-great-grandfather?'

Selim-Hassan's mother rolled her eyes. 'I pray that it isn't so,' she said.

Selim-Hassan's great-great-great-great-grandfather, the first Selim-Hassan, had been a pirate. He had sailed the oceans of the world wrecking ships and collecting thousands of shiny objects so that he could see his reflection any time he felt the need. It was Selim-Hassan's great-great-great-great-grandfather who had brought the splendid gilt-edged mirror, decorated with golden roses, back to the village in a treasure chest, together with the silver razors. He never used the razors; he spent his days admiring his wonderfully luxuriant black and curly beard in the splendid gilt-edged mirror and singing loud piratical songs.

When Selim-Hassan the Seventh began to ask questions about this less than illustrious ancestor his father shook his head. 'He was not a man to be proud of,' Selim-Hassan the Sixth said firmly. 'It is not a good thing to be a thief. You, my son, will not be like him. Our family has been waiting for you for seven generations. You will be famous for being the first among us ever to achieve the perfect shave with only seven swift swoops of the silver razor.' And Selim-Hassan the Sixth smiled hopefully at the Seventh.

Selim-Hassan the Seventh shuffled his feet and said nothing. He found his lessons in soaping and lathering and foaming tedious. He much preferred to slip away and play marbles with his friends under the shady palm trees by the well.

Days and weeks and months went past. Selim-Hassan's father began to teach him the art of shaving, and he found that even more boring than soaping and lathering. At least when he was slapping white foam on to a customer's face he could flick the lather high in the air and catch it on the end of his nose, or send a fleet of bubbles floating out of the window to sparkle in the sunshine. When he was bent over a whiskery chin holding a sharp gleaming silver razor he had to concentrate extremely hard. His father continually told him that it was not good for business to send customers out of the shop dripping gouts of blood. Selim-Hassan pulled a face at his father's back and invented his own ways of putting off the time when he would have to take his place as the village barber.

As the weeks went on, the long queue of young men, old men, fat men and thin men outside the barber's shop grew shorter. Some days there were only three or four customers. Men in the village were growing beards for the first time in living memory; day by day more and more whiskers and moustaches and beards could be seen. The barber wrung his hands in despair. He begged Selim-Hassan to try harder, but Selim-Hassan the Seventh just went on flicking his marbles in the air and catching them.

The day before Selim-Hassan's fourteenth birthday was a particularly bad day. Selim-Hassan tipped dirty water over the first customer's new white shirt. He dropped the soap and the second customer slipped and cracked his head on the porcelain sink. The towels he brought for the third customer were so hot that the man leapt out of the chair screaming. He spilt foam all over the floor. He blew bubbles out of the window instead of sweeping up, and he blunted two of the shining silver razors by sharpening them upside down.

'Selim-Hassan,' said his father. 'You will stay here tonight in the shop after we close. You will sweep the floor and clean it and polish until it shines... and you will not come home until your tasks are done.'

Selim-Hassan sighed. 'If you say so, Father,' he said, and blew another bubble.

When Selim-Hassan was alone in the shop he picked up the broom, and then put it away again. 'There's plenty of time for that,' he thought, and sitting himself down in the customer's chair he took a couple of marbles out of his pocket and began flicking them this way and that. He looked at himself in the splendid gilt-edged mirror decorated with golden roses, and winked.

Suddenly—

Clatter clatter! The marbles fell to the floor. Selim-Hassan's eyes popped wide open as he stared at the splendid gilt-edged mirror. Something was happening to his reflection... something very strange. His hair was growing. His nose was growing. His eyes were deepening... and lines were appearing on his forehead. His chin sprouted stubble... then whiskers... then a full-blown black and curly beard. A golden earring shone brightly in his left ear.

Selim-Hassan clutched at his own ears – there was nothing there. He felt his chin. It was still smooth. He had no beard. He stared transfixed at the mirror. The bearded reflection inside the gilt-edged frame stared back, and then spat loudly. Selim-Hassan's heart jumped into his mouth as a slimy wet blob landed by his foot.

'So!' growled the reflection. 'YOU are Selim-Hassan the Seventh!'

Selim-Hassan nodded. He couldn't say a word. His mouth was as dry as dust.

The reflection began to chuckle. 'Well well well! After all these generations of mealy-mouthed hardworking lily-livered barbers, I finally find a descendant who takes after ME!'

'Er...' Selim-Hassan's voice quavered. 'Er... who are you?'

The reflection raised an eyebrow. 'Me? Why, Selim-Hassan the First, of course. And delighted to have the opportunity of meeting such a nasty little hairless worm as you. Oh, yes, my boy! You may think you have ideas – but just you wait!'

Selim-Hassan the Seventh began to shake. 'I'm not all bad,' he said.

Selim-Hassan the First roared with black-toothed laughter. 'Why!' he said, 'yesterday you nearly cut the spicemixer's throat!'

Selim-Hassan gulped. He thought that nobody had seen the moment when his hand slipped. The wound had, luckily, been only a minor one.

'And,' his piratical ancestor went on, 'I've seen you slide soap up the schoolmaster's nose.' Selim-Hassan felt himself begin to blush. It had been fun watching the schoolmaster sneeze and sneeze and sneeze... and he had only done it once. Or was it twice?

'Four times,' said the pirate, reading his mind. 'And the baker found a bald patch shaved on the top of his head. The gravedigger went home with only one eyebrow. The butcher had foam in his ears and couldn't hear for a week... and THAT is why they have all decided to go away and grow beards. Soon every man in the village will do the same... and your mother and father will starve. And –' Selim-Hassan the First reached out a long arm and whacked his great-great-great-great-grandson on the back '– I have plans. GREAT plans! I'll teach you to be a pirate, my boy. We'll raze this village to the ground – and then we'll go to sea! Oh, I've been watching and waiting for this day for a long long long time.'

Then to Selim-Hassan the Seventh's complete and

utter horror his great-great-great-great-grandfather swung a stout leg over the edge of the frame and began to squeeze himself through, cursing terrible curses as he did so.

Selim-Hassan's stomach was churning, and his mind was racing. How could he stop this terrifying ancestor of his from wrecking his father's shop… and the whole village? He didn't want to be a pirate. Water made him ill. And it was one thing to play a few tricks on his father's customers – but to leave his family starving? To raze the village to the ground? Selim-Hassan the Seventh felt weak at the knees.

Meanwhile his ancestor was grunting and straining to heave his huge shoulders through the gilt-edged frame. 'Here, worm,' he snarled. 'Help me!'

A wild thought leapt into Selim-Hassan's mind. He leant forward. 'I hope you're bringing your sword, great-great-great-great-grandfather,' he said. 'And don't forget your treasure chest!'

The massive figure of the pirate stopped for a moment, puffing hard. 'My sword!' he said.

'And the treasure chest,' said Selim-Hassan. 'We'll need that!'

Selim-Hassan the First swore a string of very nasty oaths, and began heaving himself backwards. Selim-Hassan the Seventh held his breath as the shoulders squeezed away... and the leg followed. There was a sound of ripping cloth, an expletive, and the frame was clear.

Selim-Hassan the Seventh rushed towards the mirror. He tugged and pulled, but it was firmly fixed to the wall. Gasping from his efforts Selim-Hassan stepped back.

Immediately the furious face of his great-great-great-great-grandfather was in front of him. His eyes were blazing, and his blackened teeth were fixed in a terrible snarl. 'Try and get rid of me, would you?' boomed the pirate, and he glared at Selim-Hassan. 'Just you wait, little worm, just you—'

Thwack! A marble hit the pirate in the middle of his forehead. His eyes bulged, and he roared such an enormous roar that the gilt cracked and the golden roses splintered.

Thwack! Another marble hit him on the end of his nose. The pirate roared again, and flung his sword out of the mirror straight at Selim-Hassan, but—

Splatt!

Selim-Hassan the Seventh, well used to dodging his father's arm, ducked, twisted, and shot his last marble straight into Selim-Hassan the First's wide open mouth. Selim-Hassan the First choked, swallowed, hiccoughed twice – and disappeared.

Selim-Hassan the Seventh collapsed on the chair. He hardly dared to look in the splendid but no longer gilt-edged mirror, but when at last he lifted his head and gave a quick glance all he could see was the usual reflection of the barber's shop… reflected in a thousand thousand tiny pieces. The mirror was shattered.

It was a long time before Selim-Hassan's father forgave him for breaking the splendid gilt-edged mirror decorated with golden roses. It wasn't until Selim-Hassan the Seventh shaved the spicemixer with exactly seven swift swoops of his shining silver razor that his father finally stretched out his arms and called him 'My son!' once more.

The spicemixer felt his chin, and peered at his reflection in the rather ordinary wooden mirror. 'Selim-Hassan the Seventh,' he said. 'This is the VERY finest shave that I have ever had.'

Selim-Hassan the Seventh bowed and smiled, and

laid a delightfully warm towel on the spicemixer's chin. He never even glanced at the creaky floorboard by the door. There was no need for anyone else ever to know that under the floorboard were seven glass marbles and a pirate's cutlass.

*Melvin Burgess*

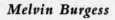

WHOSE FACE DO YOU SEE?

*Illustration by Sarah Young*

## Melvin Burgess

### WHOSE FACE DO YOU SEE?

*I don't know what I am. Not a person. Not a picture, although
a lot of people look at me. Perhaps I am a window, or a
decoration, or even a mirror.*

*People come in and out of the room where I lay. I can't move
so I don't see them very well but sometimes, someone comes up
close in front of me and then I can see them properly. There's a
woman with a fat little face and short black hair who's always*

*staring at me. For a while I thought she was looking at me, but
actually she is looking at herself. That's why I wonder if maybe
I am a mirror. Once, after she'd been looking very closely at me,
she turned round and said to someone else, 'I look and look at
her, but all I ever see is my own face.'*

*She's always holding things up in front of me – a teddy
bear, a CD cover, clothes, photographs of people. She gets very
talkative sitting next to me, although there's no one here to talk
to. There's someone she's looking for called Marianne. She calls
for Marianne over and over again. I'd like to tell her that
Marianne isn't here. There's no one here.*

*But I can't speak.*

Hospitals have always made me anxious. All those ill
people! Surely if you go into a hospital you'll fall ill and
die yourself. I remember as a child going with my
mother to a hospital – we were visiting someone, I can't
remember who – and we walked past a sign saying
*infectious diseases*. I asked Mum what infectious meant
and she told me—

'It means an illness other people catch easily,' she
said, and I thought, Oh! If you went down there you'd
be risking your life.

This hospital is different. It's not me that I'm scared for this time. Now I know that the worse things don't happen to you – they happen to your children. Ant said to me, 'When the children bury the parents, that's natural. But when the parents bury the children, that's tragedy.'

Marianne is already buried, deep inside herself where no one can dig her up.

The hospital is warm and smells of disinfectant and boiled cabbage – school meals' smell. I trot briskly down the corridor. I've been coming here for so long now it doesn't feel strange any more. It's like a second home.

Sister Charlene is on duty. 'Any change today?' I ask.

'Just the same.'

She leads the way briskly to the room where Marianne lies, opens the door and walks cheerfully up to the bed.

'Good colour today. Rosy cheeks! Nice and healthy,' she says.

It's true. Her cheeks are a bright, pretty red, as if she's been out for a crisp walk.

'Well, I'll leave you to it. Cup of tea? Yes? I'll get one sent in. Good luck. Goodbye, Marianne,' says Sister

Charlene. She always says goodbye to Marianne like that. It's good manners. For a long time the doctors told us it was possible that Marianne could hear every word. I don't think anyone believes that any more – not even me and Ant. But we have to be careful, just in case.

I put the Spice Girls on the CD player. I'm teasing, really. Marianne always loved to be teased, it used to make her shriek. If she were here now she'd shriek like a kettle and say, 'No Mum, not them, they're for babies, I never listen to them any more, you know that!'

Yes, but you used to, Marianne. Do you remember? You used to know every song backwards. You and Jill and Zoë used to do the dance routines. It was only three years ago, and already you think you were a baby then.

I hold up the CD cover.

'Remember?' I ask her.

Marianne lies with her head pushed a little back into the pillow, her eyes half open, her mouth ajar like a door. Tubes go into her mouth and up her nose. She never even flinches.

'Remember?' I ask again. I hold her hand. 'Give a little squeeze if you can hear me,' I say. I wait. Maybe it'll take a long time for the muscles to move. She has to find them again. The doctors have said that if she ever comes back to us, it will start in a tiny way, so little you might almost not notice it. So I wait. I close my eyes. I try to feel the slightest, tiny pressure on my fingers, but there's never any response.

'Remember?' I beg. 'Please, Marianne. Can you hear me?' Nothing. I bend and kiss her.

I would give everything I have for her to kiss me back.

I sit waiting for my tea, stroking her face, her arm, her hands.


*Something happened today. I had a memory. I never had one of those before.*

*It began with the woman, the sad one who comes in every day to stare at her reflection in my eyes.*

*'Marianne, Marianne, can you hear me? Can you hear me? Marianne, Marianne…'*

*What do you want? Why can't you leave me alone? I don't know who this Marianne person is – why does she keep calling me by her name? Perhaps she's teasing me. If I could, I'd block her out altogether. But it's nice to feel her warm breath on my face. She touches me with her cold hand. Sometimes she remembers to warm her hands on her breath before she touches my cheek. Then one time, she put her head close to mine so our cheeks were touching, and she lay like that, gently against me, for so long that I think I fell asleep, and that's when I had my memory.*

*This is my memory. I was lost. I can't remember how I got lost, I think I'd just wandered away too far. I remember tall houses behind the hedgerow. I remember the road, which was dark and speckled with little white and brown stones, and I had no idea how to get home.*

*Then I was in a house with some people who must have taken me in. One of them asked me if I wanted something to eat, and although I was hungry I was too shy to accept, so I said no. Then, my mum came to fetch me, and I was so happy, so happy to see her. I ran to her when she came into the room and flung my arms around her, and I can remember smiling and smiling and smiling at her, endlessly smiling, I was so happy to have her back. She was trying to be cross but she was smiling too, because I was so happy, and all the people in the room at the table were smiling at me, because I was so, so happy to have my mum back...*

*Then I realised what all this is about. Once upon a time, you see, I was a person, too. I was a girl called Marianne. I had a mother. The woman with the black hair — you see? A father — the small man she calls Ant who smells of cigarettes who comes in with her sometimes. And who knows? Brothers and sisters and friends.*

*It was long ago. Then something happened. The woman, the mother, thinks that I'm still Marianne. Poor woman! I wish I could tell her that Marianne is gone. Once I was, but then something happened and I got turned into this instead.*

'I don't believe she's in any pain,' says Dr Morris patiently.

I nod, but I can't get it out of my mind. What if she's lying there in agony, day after day, week after week, month after month? And she can't say a word.

'The real question is not if she's in any pain, but whether or not she's ever going to wake up. It's been eight months now,' says Dr Morris. 'Physically she's perfectly healthy, but we have no evidence of any personality at all.'

My Marianne. She's perfectly healthy but she has no personality. And now the hospital has had enough. There are so many patients and not enough staff, not enough beds, not enough doctors. Of course, she has a right to life, but there is an alternative. We can simply withdraw support. No drugs to kill her, but no medicines to fight off infection, and no food and drink to sustain her. She would be heavily sedated, there would be no discomfort – assuming she is capable of discomfort, which none of us believe any more anyway. She would pass quietly away without any fuss or distress within a week.

Ant squeezes my hand. We've talked about this before. We knew it was coming. Probably it's the right thing to do.

Probably is a big word.

Ant clears his throat. The doctor looks up.

'What are the chances that she might come round after so long?' he wants to know.

'Very small.' The doctor shakes his head. 'Brain activity is very low. I would be most surprised if there was ever any improvement. In our opinion...'

'In your opinion, she should die.' My voice jars in the little consultation office. Doctor Morris purses his lips.

'In my opinion, Marianne is already dead, Mrs Sams. At this stage, we're just making a recommendation. The decision is yours. I understand how painful this must be.'

Ant nods. 'While there's life, there's hope,' he says.

The doctor bows his head. 'In this case very little hope, I'm afraid.'

'But there is some,' I insist.

'Very little,' he repeats.

Ant and I nod, like dogs in the back of a car.

We go into her room and watch her. Is that my daughter? Is there anyone here apart from us? While there's life there's hope, but hope can be cruel. What about the rest of us? Our son, Simon. Poor child, he's had little enough of my attention this past year. The strain is crushing us. Marianne is silently ruining our lives. The coma goes on and on and on. She is not my daughter any more. She is, to put it bluntly, a vegetable.

I sit on the bed and hold up her things. Her little tank top. Do you remember, Marianne? Nana bought you this, you wore it until it got so tight it looked ridiculous and I had to hide it from you. Her necklace of wild pearls. Do you remember this Marianne? Marianne? Marianne? Please wake up darling...

'Marianne, wake up, Marianne, wake up! You have to wake up, darling, please, it's getting very late. Marianne!'

Ant takes my arm. I'm shouting.

'She can't hear you, Julie.'

I stand up. I take a breath.

'We can't be sure.'

'We can never be sure. But.'

'Give her another week. One week.'

He smiles. 'A bit longer than that, perhaps. There's no hurry.'

'We've waited this long.'

'It's her birthday next month. Let's wait for that.'


*Why one month? Why not two or three? Why not forever?*

*It's all so far, far away. Mum? Are you still there? You see, I'd like to come back, even if it was just to say goodbye. But I can't quite make it.*

*I can remember a lot now. I can remember her, my mother. I can remember my father and Simon, and my friends. I remember the music she plays and the things she shows to me, over and over again. They used to belong to Marianne.*

*What I can't remember is myself. It's just like the doctor says — I'm not here. I'm like a mirror. I reflect things — my mother, my teddy bear, my CDs, my clothes. But I'm gone. I can't remember who Marianne was. I can't remember who she used to be, what she used to do, or feel or think. I can't remember her face. I can't remember anything about her. Marianne's body is here — her memories are here — but she has gone forever.*

*I have no present. I have no future. I only have a past.*

*I'd like to tell them that it's right. Marianne would agree if she were here. She wouldn't want everyone to keep coming into the hospital, year after year, watch her get older and older. So yes, please. Turn me off, pull out my tubes. I've done nothing but lie here for all this time and I'm still so, so tired. I just want it to stop.*

*Another month. It's more than enough for me.*

Ant and I are clopping along the corridors, surrounded by people. We're carrying armfuls of streamers and balloons, and plastic boxes full of sausage rolls, jelly and other goodies.

Hospitals are always so quiet. Hush, people are ill, don't make any noise. But today is different. Today Marianne is thirteen years old. She's going out with a bang.

The doctors didn't terribly approve. A party in a hospital? Loud music? Friends, dancing? Well… there are other people in here, you know. Sick people…

But it makes me feel better. We've got used to the

idea that she's gone; now we just want to celebrate her life. Happy birthday Marianne! Goodbye, darling. Look, Simon is here, and Nana and Granddad and Jill and Zoë. They didn't let us bring Daisy the cat – animals in the ward were just too much – but everyone else is here. Who knows, if we make enough noise, maybe we'll wake you up.

Open the door. There she is, head pushed back as always. All together now…

'Happy Birthday, Marianne!'


*Happy Birthday, Marianne!*

*It was a good party. They all enjoyed themselves – well, they looked as if they did, anyway. Now, Mum and Dad are sitting on my bed, each holding a hand. There are streamers all over the bed, balloons rolling on the floor. They popped so many that the nurse came in and said we'd give the other patients a heart attack if we made any more noise. There was a cake with candles, there was jelly and sausage rolls. We played the music really loud! Jill and Zoë did a dance around the room and nearly knocked the heart monitor over. Mum and Dad turned out the lights and lit the candles and everyone sang Happy Birthday, and they blew the candles out for Marianne.*

*Marianne would have enjoyed it. It's a pity she couldn't come.*

*Yes, I know. I've let you all down. I didn't dance or sing, I didn't even blink. But I did enjoy it. I wish I could say.*

'Goodbye, darling. I'm so, so sorry. Goodbye.'

'Goodbye, Marianne.'

'Goodbye.'

*Yes, goodbye, Mum, goodbye Dad! It was good of you to try for so long. I'm sorry, but the doctor's right; Marianne isn't here. It's just this old shell and these old memories. They look the same, but they don't mean anything, really.*

*But poor old Mum, she has to try. One last time. Here she goes again, holding the things up before me. Teddy bear, clothes, CDs. Picture of Marianne with her mum and dad. Picture of Marianne dancing with Jill and Zoë. Poor Marianne. Poor Mum and Dad! Tonight they take the tubes out. It won't hurt, they've told them that. It's the best thing.*

*Mum stands up. She puts the things back in the box by the side of the bed. She straightens the photographs by the bedside. Marianne would be happy, but she's gone away, Mrs Sams. Honestly. I'll give her your love if I see her where I'm going.*

'We'd better go.'

*Yes, Mum, go. It's all for the best.*

*But although my dad is saying let's go, he isn't going himself. He has something in his hand.*

'Worth a try. We haven't tried this for a while.' *And my dad moves something in front of me.*

*It's a mirror. At least, I think it's a mirror, but perhaps it's not. Because in the mirror is a picture of Marianne.*

'Darling, look. It's you.'

*It's Marianne.*

'It's you, darling. Marianne, can you see?'

*No, it's not me. It's Marianne.*

'Can you see, Marianne?'

*Is it? Is it me? Am I... ?*


'She moved, Julie, look, she moved! Her mouth moved!'

*I never move.*

'Are you sure? It's your imagination.'

*I can't blink, I can't move. I'm not here...*

'She moved, I saw her! God! Marianne, do it again – look. Oh, Lord, do it again for your mother, darling. See, that's you, that's you there in the mirror. Just smile, darling, just do it again – oh, please, please, I know I saw you... just try to smile, Marianne.'

*Like this...*

'Oh my God, she moved. She tried to smile. Oh, God! God God God!'

'Marianne! It's really you…'

*Is that really me? Was that me all the time? Really? I never dreamt that was me…*

*Now Mum grabs hold of my hand.* 'Squeeze Marianne, squeeze hard if you can hear me.' *And Dad's shouting and jumping around the room, and I want to cry too, because it really is me, you know. I saw it – I moved my mouth!*

*The door opens and the doctor comes in.*

'What is it?'

'She moved. She tried to smile. She moved!'

'That's not possible.'

*The doctor comes to the bed and leans over into my face. MY face. There is a long pause while I look around for the muscles. Where have they gone?*

'Take her hand. Take her hand. Marianne, squeeze. Squeeze for the doctor. Marianne, please?'

*I can feel his hand resting in mine. I squeeze.*

Hello doctor. I'm Marianne. I just found out.

## Celia Rees

### SILVER LAUGHTER

*Illustration by Sarah Young*

## *Celia Rees*

### Silver Laughter

The Hadley place lay deep in the woods. No one knew for sure who the Hadleys were, or when they'd lived there, or why they'd left, but it must have been long ago. The garden was full of waist-high weeds; the shrubs and bushes had turned into trees. The roof had begun to shed its tiles. They hung down like huge, black leaves and littered the ground below. The house was not boarded

115

up. There was nothing to stop the vandals invading, or the weather from following them. The front door was twisted back on one rusty hinge and the downstairs windows were all smashed in. Only a few upper storey panes, just out of stone-throwing range, still clung, bleary with age, to their black rotten frames.

Inside, sections of wood panelling had sprung away from the walls and paper hung down like peeling skin. There were things, family things, in some of the rooms. Most of the portable stuff had been carted away, but some of the furniture still remained, giving an air of warped normality, like the setting for some sinister fairy story. A sofa and chairs were grouped round the fireplace, just like in someone's home, but this three-piece was fat with damp, as soft and slimy as a clump of toadstools. The mantelpiece jutted like a bracket fungus. Above it hung a picture, permanently askew; suspended from a chain, twisted and clotted with verdigris. A squat stove stood in the hearth. One of the little doors was hanging off, the ancient coals spilling out. Its chimney had collapsed and lay broken into pieces, strewn across the floor.

The Hadley place was our own local haunted house

and there were plenty of stories about it. We used to dare each other to go inside. It wasn't really scary, just cold and clammy, and a bit smelly, but that wasn't the point. We'd crowd in, jostling and pushing, being really brave. Then something would stir, some sound would be heard...

Fear would jump like a current from one to another, and we would run, hearts thumping, elbows pumping, until we were safely away. Then we would speak in breathless whispers and tell each other what had happened.

'I saw something. I saw something, definitely.'

'And me.'

'And me.'

'Well, I heard something.'

'It has to be haunted because...'

Then the stories would start. Grisly suicide and gruesome murder. Mad men wielding axes strode through, dripping blood from room to room. Crazy women wept and wailed, before turning long curving knives on themselves. Only ghosts could live there now.

None of that was right. The real story of the house, and why it had been left like that, was far stranger than anything we could devise.

I hadn't been there for a while and I had no plans to go there now. We were twelve, and at secondary school, so playing 'Haunted House' was a bit uncool. I was walking through the woods, kind of aimlessly, I had nothing much to do that day, when I heard something. A soft musical tinkling that came and went on the wind, chiming in time to the rustling leaves. It was like nothing I'd heard in the woods before. I was drawn by it, straying further and further from the path down towards the Hadley place.

I first saw the things hanging in the holly trees which grew, tall as poplars, standing guard on either side of the place where the old garden gate had been. Something in their lower branches twisted in the breeze, flashing in my eyes, blinding me. I turned to see a lightning strike of a face staring from the opposite tree. Eye, nose, cheek. For a moment I failed to recognise myself.

Now I could see what these things were. Someone had collected fragments of mirror and tied the long jagged slivers together with scarlet thread. Someone had hung them in the trees all around, surrounding the house in a circle of light and sound, setting them to turn and shine in the sun and make that eerie music as the pieces clashed softly together.

The effect was strange, hypnotising. I walked down the path as if in a dream, beckoned by mirror fingers signalling to me from the empty window of the house.

A girl lay curled up on the sofa. I hardly dared to breathe, fearing that I might wake her. I wasn't all that surprised to see someone there. The place had shown signs of use before. The blackened remains of fires stained the flagstone floor. Bottles, cans and cigarette butts lay amongst the drifts of twigs and leaves; litter left by kids holding Hallowe'en parties, or tramps and the homeless who drifted here from town. I just thought the girl was one of those. She looked harmless enough. Anyway, I thought I'd seen her before…

'Pretty, aren't they?' She pointed up at the chimes. 'What do you think?'

I nodded.

'I made them.'

I nodded again.

'Won't you come in?'

I stepped through the window. Tiny shards and nuggets of glass crunched under foot and glittered like diamonds all the way to the hearth. On the wall above the fireplace was a clean oval space. I'd thought before that a painting hung there with the canvas cut out. Now I saw it had been a mirror, turned to show its plywood back. The frame lay on the floor, the centre smashed out, little bits stuck to the rim like jagged mirror teeth around an open mouth. She must have broken it to make the chimes.

'Isn't it seven years bad luck?'

She shrugged. 'I've had that times five.'

She leaned forward, her hair falling down like a curtain. The natural colour showed fair at the tips, but the rest hung lank, darkened by dirt and grease to a grubby mud brown. She swept the stringy lengths back, pinning them with bony fingers, stretching the skin on a face already skull-like and thin. She stared at me. Her eyes were a pale washed-out blue. The shadows around them made her look older, but I was sure I'd seen her.

'Don't I know you?'

'I don't think so.'

'I'm sure I've seen your picture...'

*Description: Carole-Anne is fifteen years old. She is small of stature, with blonde hair and blue eyes. She was last seen wearing white trainers, blue flared jeans and a pink jumper...*

This girl was dressed in a matted jumper which could once have been pink and her jeans flared out over thin dirty ankles. Her feet were bare, but the trainers could be somewhere. Carole-Anne Donaldson. It had to be her. She had disappeared several weeks ago. Set off on a trip to the shops and hadn't come back. I'd seen her picture on the telly, on posters. The image had been a little blurred, and she'd looked younger, as though they'd used an old picture, but the likeness was close enough. I'd seen her parents, white-faced and tense, pleading for her to come home to them. I thought about my parents, how they'd feel if I just disappeared like that. That's why I stayed. I thought to get her talking, maybe persuade her to come back with me.

'Why did you do it?'

'Do what?'

'Run away.'

'Because I was scared. Isn't that why anyone runs away from anything?'

I didn't reply. I was trying to think what could be scary enough to make me want to run away from my mum, my dad, my family.

'I thought they'd blame me.'

Guilt could do it. Guilt, or shame. Maybe she'd had a bad report from school, or had been found out doing something bad.

'Blame you for what?'

'For what happened.'

She looked around the ruined room.

'I thought they'd looked for you here.'

I seem to remember Dad mentioning that. I think he even went on the search.

'Of course they did.'

'Why did you come back, then?'

'I had to.'

'For what?'

I still didn't get it. I just thought she'd left something. She seemed so normal, so ordinary. Dirty and tired-looking, pale and thin, but I put that down to not enough food and not enough sleep. A real girl could get that way, if she was living rough, if she was homeless.

'To make amends for what I had done.'

It was only then that I began to think: this is not Carole-Anne *anyone*.

'I didn't do it on purpose,' she went on, not looking at me, not looking at anything in the room with us now.

'I left them in here asleep, the twins on the sofa, the baby in his crib. I thought they were asleep. They looked so peaceful, I didn't want to disturb them. The baby had been crying all night, keeping everyone awake. Dad had gone off to work, Mum to the shops, leaving me in charge. It was cold, so I put more coke in the stove, so it'd be snug and warm for them, then I went out. I wasn't going far, just for a bit of a walk. Then I came back...' she stopped and turned around, focusing on the place where bits of the old stove lay rusting on the ground. 'When I came back, they were just as I left them, cheeks all rosy. I thought they looked bonny. That's what I thought. That's all I thought.' Her lips were white. She wiped her mouth on the back of her hand as if she wanted to rub the colour back into them. 'It took me a while to realise... then I did what was necessary. What was fitting.'

'What would that be?'

She glanced up at the pale patch above the fireplace.

'I turned the mirror. That's what you do when death comes to the house. Didn't you know that?'

I shook my head. I didn't trust myself to speak. I was beginning to feel a little sick.

'They were dead, you see, dead even before I went out, already poisoned, choked on the fumes from the stove. I did what was fitting, and then I left. I haven't been back since.'

'When was that?' My words came out small and flat. 'When did you go?'

'I told you, five times seven.'

'Thirty-five years ago?'

She thought, as if calculating in her head. 'More or less.'

'Why didn't you come back before?'

'I didn't know.'

'Know what?'

'That what I'd done was wrong. I left them trapped, trapped up there in the mirror. I couldn't leave them like that. I had to free them. Let them out.'

She got up and went to the window. She did not flinch and her feet made no sound as she stepped on the glass carpeting the ground.

'See that?' A fragment of mirror twisted in the wind, catching the sun, blinding both of us. 'That's them waving goodbye. Hear that?' Her hand brushed the shards. They clashed together in a cascading fall, chiming like wordless voices, twisting and coming together again in an eerie chuckling, echoey and metallic. 'That's them saying goodbye. I'm going to join them. Would you like to come, too?'

She smiled and came gliding back, her wrinkle-skinned hand reaching out, curling towards me like a grasping bird claw...

I fled, leaping through the empty window, running down the path, thrashing through the brambles and weeds that grabbed at my feet and ankles. My shoulder caught the bunch of glass suspended from the holly tree, setting the shards spinning out and away from me. I tried to dodge as they came swinging back, but a splinter caught my cheek, parting the skin in a thin line of red. Then I was past them and off, leaving them chiming and peeling in my wake. I didn't stop running until I was home and safe.

Carole-Anne Donaldson was found the very next day, picked up by the police in some town miles away. I haven't been near the Hadley place since; but I still walk through the woods sometimes. When I do, I have a feeling as though I'm not alone; and everywhere I go, I'm followed by the sound of silver laughter.

*Anne Fine*

Use It or Lose It

*Illustration by Tim Stevens*

## Anne Fine

### Use It or Lose It

So I'm off for my session with Mr Holdcroft. Most people see him in town, but since he has two offices, and my school is halfway between, on Tuesdays he calls in. We meet in the interview room or, if someone's in there, in the first empty classroom. Usually I miss English, but today it was Geography, so I put my hand up early and spent the extra time hanging about in front of the mirror in the old changing rooms.

Which was about as stupid as can be, since that's what I was sent to him for in the first place.

Staring in mirrors.

Mirrors have haunted me since I was four or five years old. That's when, staring in one, I first had the feeling I could see someone staring back. My face, of course. My clothes. My hair. The very room that I was standing in, even if back to front.

But not me. No, not me.

It's in the eyes. You stand, grave-faced, and look at your reflection. But that's not you who's gazing levelly back. It's someone else. Not quite a stranger, since it's obvious that nothing about you will surprise. (This person, after all, does know you backwards.)

But someone you don't know.

Creepy. Especially since it never happens when you're with friends, or in a rush. Then, either you're hurrying past, checking only the basics like whether you dripped spaghetti down yourself over lunch and if you're buttoned up right. Or, if there are friends either side of you, laughing and chatting, it's their eyes that you seek out in the glass, and not your own.

When you're alone, it's different. When I was small, I used to drag the old fringed piano stool across the rug until it was in front of the fireguard. I'd shut the door, to give myself those vital few handle-rattling seconds of warning in case anyone came in. And then I'd clamber up. My face appeared above the party invitations and the china thimbles, and the shallow black lacquer dish in which my family drop stray buttons, mislaid cuff links, foreign coins.

And I would stare.

And, in a moment, there was someone staring back who wasn't me. You know. You blink, and so do they. You twitch your nose. They twitch theirs. You make a complicated horrid face. They make it perfectly back, and all exactly at the very same time.

But still you know.

That was the year the easy sleeping stopped. Night after night I'd force myself to stay awake. I'd lie for hours, keeping my eyes wide open to watch the shadows in the corner, for fear those dark and threatening shapes would spring to life. In the end, desperate, I'd push back the covers and make a headlong, terrified, dash to the door to find that, in the slice of light that flooded in, those peaked ears and that searching snout became a crumpled pair of jeans dropped out of sight and mind.

Later, I got it in my head there was a devil on my pillow. He wasn't banished by the light. Or by the comforters, who came when I hollered and sat on my bed.

'Devil? What sort of devil?'

'I'm not sure.'

'What does he look like?'

'I don't know. I've never seen him. He can move so fast that, by the time I've turned my head, he's on the other side.'

'And yet you're sure he's there?'

Not quite sure, I'd have liked to have been able to explain. Just sure enough not to be able to sleep safely.

I'm not so bothered by the devil now. But still I just can't sleep. And there is still this thing with mirrors. Now that I'm older, I don't need the stool. But I still have to stare in every mirror if I'm on my own. Can't tear myself away. I'm out to catch my mirror image in one small mistake. Prove to myself I'm right. I stop and watch. Lift a hand – fast. Blink fiercely. (That one is hard to check. How could you tell?) Stick out my tongue. Everything I do, the ghost in the mirror does perfectly.

And the eyes never falter.

Cunning, I think. And then: I'll catch you out! Don't think I'm such a fool. Our eyes may share a colour, but yours are – oh, so different. They're cold and knowing. Watchful. Not like mine.

That's when I look beyond to search for clues. Over the stranger's shoulder, I study the room. Again, the same but different. And so much more intriguing and inviting, now that the window's on the other side, and the girl in the painting is facing the other way. Even the plants seem somehow to trail more interestingly out of their pots when they do it contrariwise.

What's that? That's not been there before. That must be—

I spin round. But I'm wrong. The letter that I've spotted is lying, spread out, on the sideboard behind me. And anyway, it's not the sort of elementary mistake this stranger staring so coolly would ever make. I turn back to those dead eyes, that absence of expression. The vigilance makes me uneasy. After I step away, will they still be watching?

'Obsessing', Mr Holdcroft calls it. 'Unwanted and repetitive thoughts'. 'A sort of mental interference that stops you getting on with life'.

I called it 'haunted'. I asked my brothers once. 'George,' I said, finding him first. 'What do you see when you look in the mirror?'

He looked up from the sleeping bag he was patching. 'Is this a riddle?'

'No.'

He shrugged. 'Then, me, I suppose.'

'Always you? *Just* you?'

'Well,' he said thoughtfully. 'Sometimes for a moment I used to think it was Eddie. Until I moved. And then I'd realise that it must be me.'

Then I asked Eddie. 'If you just happened to be staring in a mirror, what would you see?'

'George,' he said promptly. 'Until I notice he's not making a stupid face. And then I know it's my reflection.'

They're twins, though. They would see things differently. But just because each of my brothers has a living image of himself, why should I get it in my head I have one too, behind the glass?

So, picture me, standing there waiting for Mr Holdcroft in front of the long mirror that runs the whole way down the changing room, across from the sign that says, YOUR HEALTHY BODY – YOU USE IT OR LOSE IT. The glass is old and pockmarked – even blurred. You have the feeling, when you look in it, that it could melt, and you could let yourself be drawn through, into that strange looking-glass land where doors lead off on the wrong side and what's through a window looks sharper and richer.

The eyes are there already, watching me. I'm not quite ready. I look down, at my chewed nails, my raw fingers. I take a breath and look up. Now I can see what Mum meant when she said the shadows under my eyes were turning to pitch.

The eyes wait.

'Who *are* you?' I want to ask. 'What do you *want*? What are you *thinking*?'

Really, the question's: 'Friend or foe?' Except I know the answer, because I'm the only person in the year who has to waste an hour each week with Mr Holdcroft in the quest for sleep.

'Why *me*?' I plead. 'Why pick on me? I'm nothing special. All that I want to do is stop yawning long enough to get through my classes.'

And yet the eyes stare back so deeply into mine that it's as clear as paint whoever it is that's watching knows better.

Then suddenly, behind the two of us, is Mrs Tallentire, who'll teach me English next year.

'What are you doing in here, out of class?'

'Waiting. Waiting for Mr Holdcroft.'

'Mr Holdcroft?'

Then she remembers.

Mostly, after a meeting like this, whichever teacher it is can't melt away, embarrassed, fast enough. ('Oh, right then. Jolly good. Back into class just as soon as you're ready.')

Not her. She comes to stand at my side in front of the mirror.

'So who were you talking to?'

And, mostly, I'd die a thousand deaths rather than mutter anything except, 'No one.' But I'm so tired – of myself, of this. And she's so welcome, plump and colourful in her daisy frock, banishing the silence and even managing to cut that other weird, bleak, back-to-front cloakroom I can see in the mirror down to flat glass.

Instead, I hear myself telling her, 'I'm not sure.'

She's seeking out my eyes now.

'Touch of the ghost in the mirror?'

How does she *know*?

'Well, well,' she says. 'And do you get the living shadows in the bedroom, too, after the light's out?'

'Not any more,' I told her.

'And what about the goblin behind you on the pillow – the one that moves so fast that, if you swing your head around, it's already jumped to the other side?'

'Devil,' I corrected. 'I see him as having piercing fiery red eyes and sharp black claws.'

'Imaginary friends?' she asked.

'Yes,' I admitted.

'Long conversations with invisible strangers?'

'All the time.'

'Toys with real feelings?'

'Well, not so much any more, of course. Except for my—'

But she's not after the details. 'Thoughts of death?'

I nod.

'Imagine lying in your coffin?'

'Yes.'

'Nibbled by worms?'

'I'd considered cremation,' I told her.

'Right,' she said, satisfied. 'I shall look forward to having someone like you in my classes.' Her eyes narrowed in suspicion. 'What are you missing now?'

'Geography,' I said hastily.

'Fine,' she said, moving off like some giant bright flowerbed under sail. 'Just so long as it's not English.'

And she was gone.

The doors swung closed behind. I stood and waited till the creaking stopped. Then I turned back to the mirror in which the last half of the sign on the other wall was blotchily reflected.

USE IT OR LOSE IT

I've read it a million times over. But, this time, like everything else in a mirror, it seemed to be offering something different, something far more intriguing and inviting.

And, this time, my own reflection in the mirror didn't bother me. I don't think I was even really watching. I think I was trying to work out the most gentle way of telling Mr Holdcroft I don't think I'll be coming very much longer.

Because I really don't believe I will.

*Paul Stewart*

DOUBLE VISION

*Illustration by Sarah Young*

## Paul Stewart

### DOUBLE VISION

'This is terrible!' Craig heard his mum complaining.

Outside, the fog was thicker than ever. The motorway traffic was crawling along, lights blazing. After two wonderful weeks in the Lakes, the return journey was turning into a nightmare.

Molly and Liz, Craig's two younger sisters, were asleep beside him on the back seat. Up front, his dad was hunched over the steering wheel, while beside him, his mum peered grimly out of the window.

'Let's leave at the next junction and find somewhere to spend the night.' she suggested. 'Hopefully, the fog will have lifted by morning.'

'Good idea,' said his father.

Half an hour later, the five of them were clustered together in front of a large desk in the entrance hall of Knottley Manor Hotel.

'You're in luck, Mr Burgess,' said the receptionist, looking up. 'There's a family suite free for the one night.'

'Ideal,' said Craig's dad. 'We'll take it.'

The receptionist handed him a key. 'Third floor,' she said. 'Number thirteen.'

'Thir*teen*,' Craig heard Molly whisper to Liz, as they climbed the stairs. 'That's unlucky, that is. I bet you there's a ghost.'

'A ghost!' gasped Liz.

'It's such an old place,' said Molly. 'There's bound to be. What do you think, Craig?'

Craig snorted. 'I think you're both nutters,' he said. He wasn't about to admit that he, too, had been wondering whether the old sprawling manor might be haunted.

Their suite was made up of two bedrooms, a sitting room and a bathroom. The rooms were all small, and made smaller still by the huge dark furniture which filled them. Mr Burgess checked his watch.

'Bedtime, you lot,' he said. 'Molly, Liz; you're in the room with the twin beds. We'll take the double bed. Craig, the bed-settee out here for you, I'm afraid.'

'That's fine, Dad,' said Craig. After two weeks of sharing with his sisters, a room on his own sounded perfect.

He wasn't so sure, later. As he lay in the strange bed with its cold sheets and heavy blankets, the room creaked and groaned with unfamiliar noises, Craig began to feel uneasy. He looked round, and his gaze came to rest on the mirror on the wall opposite.

It was small, round, and set in an ornate, golden frame. Despite its size, Craig discovered that he could see every corner of the room reflected in it – the window, the doors, the fireplace and, propped up against big striped pillows, himself. Like the back of a spoon, the mirror was convex – a huge gold and silver fish-eye that seemed to be staring back into the room at him.

Craig waved his arms. His reflection waved back. He

stuck out his tongue. His reflection did the same. He leant across and switched off the bedside lamp, then closed his eyes and imagined his other self lying there on the bed-settee; still, silent, and *so* sleepy...

The voices were loud and angry. A man's voice, and a woman's voice. 'Mum? Dad?' Craig wondered drowsily. 'Is that you?'

The shouting continued, booming yet muffled. Unfamiliar. No, it was not his parents. Perhaps it was the people in the next room arguing...

Just then, there was an almighty *crash*!

Craig's eyes snapped open. He sat bolt upright, looked round — and gasped.

Something weird was going on in the convex mirror. For though Craig was in darkness, the room reflected in the glass was glowing brightly, both from the fire blazing in the grate and several candles which stood on the heavy sideboard. Suddenly the room became brighter still, as a dazzling flash of lightning filled the window.

'B... but this is impossible,' Craig breathed. 'It's...'

He stopped as he noticed something even stranger. The room in the mirror was not empty.

Two people were there: a tall, heavily-built man and a slim, pale woman with lank, fair hair twisted up in a straggly bun. The man was standing by the fireplace, rubbing round his right eye tenderly. The woman was perched on the edge of the settee, arm raised and face twisted with rage.

Craig shuddered and spun round anxiously, but there was nobody there beside him.

Back in the mirror, the man bent down and picked up a large piece of broken china. He brandished it in the air and shouted at the woman. The woman shouted back.

The words – half-echoing, half-muffled – came and went on sloshing waves of hiss. Yet there was no doubt what had happened. In the middle of their furious row, the woman must have thrown something at the man, and it had hit him.

The man stormed to the mirror, and Craig let out a startled cry as the huge, angry face abruptly filled the glass. It was as if the man's eyes were glaring straight at him.

'It's OK,' Craig told himself. 'He can't see you.'

Shouting all the while, the man inspected his face. There was a cut on his right eyebrow, and a black eye was already forming. He reached up to staunch the blood with a handkerchief. As he did so, Craig saw the tattoos on his forearms: a dragon on one, a tiger on the other. He also looked at the man's clothing more closely.

With the black frock coat, the frilled shirt and purple cravat, he looked like something out of one of those boring period dramas his mum was always watching on telly. And as he stepped away from the mirror and the woman approached him, Craig saw that she, too, was dressed in old-fashioned clothes – a long blue gown, a lace shawl.

'The clothes, the candles,' he whispered. 'Could I somehow be looking into the past?' An icy shiver ran the length of his spine. 'If I am, it means Molly was right. Knottley Manor *is* haunted.'

As the thunderstorm raged on outside, the man pointed to his eye and bellowed loudly. The woman lowered her head and replied calmly, apologetically. But the man was having none of it and, with his arms gesticulating, he ranted all the more furiously – which made the woman lose her temper again and screech back louder than ever.

Unable as he was to hear the words properly, Craig

could feel the fury that was fuelling them. And it was scary.

'Go away,' he murmured, his voice low, trembling. But the characters remained just where they were, locked in their furious argument. 'No? Then, I'll *make* you go away!'

He would unhook the mirror and put it in the bathroom – or in the corridor outside. Whatever, he would silence them once and for all. He climbed out of bed and made his way across the dark, cluttered room.

Inside the mirror, the drama continued. One moment the couple embraced; the next, they pulled away from each other angrily. Once the man shook the woman by her shoulders. Once the woman slapped the man. It was like watching some Victorian soap opera – apart from one thing. Craig knew that this was real. He was seeing something that had actually happened, and his blood ran cold as it occurred to him that the present is only ever haunted by the most gruesome of events from the past.

With his nerve beginning to fail him, Craig continued towards the mirror more slowly. What *had* happened in the room all those years ago? And did he really want to know?

All at once, the woman cried out and flung her arms around the man. He hugged her back. For a moment it looked as if the row was over. But then, as Craig stared unblinking into the mirror, the man abruptly pulled away. Eyes blazing and face contorted with rage, he shoved the woman hard.

She staggered backwards, tripped over the broken pot, tottered and fell. Her body hit the floor with a dull thud. The next moment there was a sharp *crack* as her head struck the side of the hearth.

Craig stared numbly into the mirror, scarcely able to take it all in. There was blood trickling down her cheek. Could she be dead?

Inside the mirror, the man fell to the floor and cradled the woman in his arms. He wiped away the blood. He kissed her forehead. He pressed his ear to her chest to listen for her heartbeat.

Craig moved up close to the mirror, and froze. The woman was not dead, after all. Her fingers were tightening their grip on a heavy, iron poker which lay in the hearth.

'No,' Craig breathed.

Just then, the man jumped up and seized the mirror

from the wall. Craig watched dizzily as the blurred image swayed wildly, before settling in on the woman's motionless face. The man was clearly hoping the glass would mist up.

It didn't, of course. The woman was holding her breath. But the man didn't know that, and Craig watched his face reappear as he checked the glass for himself. In an instant, his hope turned to despair. He opened his mouth and howled with grief.

Then, at the very edge of the mirror, Craig caught a sudden flash of movement. The next instant he heard the sound of splintering bone as the heavy poker slammed into the side of the man's head. A momentary look of astonishment passed over the man's features. Then his eyes glazed over. He dropped the mirror and slumped forwards. There was a muffled cry from the woman, then nothing…

The man's lifeless face came closer and closer as he tumbled down towards the fallen mirror. His head struck the frame. His face came to rest on the curved glass.

Craig stared in dumb horror at the hideously distorted face before him: the flattened nose, the twisted mouth – and one eye staring blindly back at him. As he stood there, shaking and unable to move, the whole grizzly scene was abruptly stained with red. Blood was gushing from the dead man's terrible wound.

'No! Stop it!' Craig screamed. '*Make it go away*!'

Suddenly the light came on.

'What do you think you're doing?' came his dad's voice.

'*Shush*, he's sleepwalking,' Mum whispered. 'Come back to bed, Craig.'

Still shaken, Craig let himself be led across the room and tucked up in bed. He mentioned nothing about the ghostly deaths he'd just witnessed. His parents would have tried to persuade him that it was all just a nightmare – and there had already been enough arguments in the room for one night.

'Spooky!' said Molly, the following morning.

'Scary,' said Liz.

'It was the *spookiest, scariest* thing that's *ever* happened to me,' said Craig dramatically.

The three of them were in the lobby waiting for their parents to pay the bill, and Craig was having a great time thrilling his sisters with the events of the previous night.

'I wonder when it happened?' said Molly.

'I wonder who they were?' said Liz.

'I don't know.' Craig shrugged. 'And I doubt whether I ever will. No one I've asked knows anything about any ghosts, or murders. Unless they're just not saying...'

'All set, kids?' said Dad, appearing behind them. 'The fog's cleared but there are bad thunderstorms forecast for later, so let's get going.'

As Craig followed the others past the reception desk, he thought he heard someone mention *Suite Thirteen*. He glanced round to see a young couple checking in. His heart missed a beat. The woman was slim and pale, with lank fair hair. The man was tall, dark and hefty.

No, he thought, turning away. I must be imagining it. It *can't* be them.

'I'm afraid,' the receptionist was saying, 'your rooms won't be ready until midday.'

'That's fine,' said the woman. 'I've got a bit of shopping to do. We're going to a fancy-dress ball this evening. Victorian theme. I was hoping to find a lace shawl...'

Craig froze. Then, slowly, nervously, he turned to look at them more carefully. The man had put down the suitcases and was standing with his hands on his hips. And there on his forearms were two tattoos: one dragon, one tiger.

'Come on, Craig,' his mum called.

Craig turned and walked towards her. His head was spinning. He hadn't seen into the past at all; he'd seen into the future. He wanted to do something, to say something – to warn them… But how? They'd think he was a complete nutter!

'Are you all right, love?' said his mum. 'You look as though you've just seen a ghost.'

'A ghost?' said Craig weakly. 'I wish I had.'

## Kate Thompson

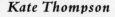

### The Dragon's Dream

*Illustration by Sarah Young*

*Kate Thompson*

## The Dragon's Dream

Once upon a time and far, far away, there was a young king who lived in a castle high up in the mountains. The king was very wealthy, and the great hall in his castle was piled high with treasure, but still he was not happy. Noblemen came and went, and there were always servants scurrying through the castle, but even so, this king was lonely. He was lonely because in all the length and breadth of his land he could find no one who would marry him.

Now, the reason that no one would marry him was that his castle was so cold. All through the winter it was covered in snow, and even during the summer, when the people in the valleys were enjoying the sunshine, icy winds blew through the castle in the mountains. So the servants scurried to keep themselves warm, and the noblemen who came soon left again because their beards froze in their beds at night and they could not bear to stay there.

Every day the track which led up from the valley was filled with peasants toiling under loads of wood for the castle fires. The forests had been cleared for miles around, but still it was not enough. The castle just could not be heated. The king worked hard and was a kind and just ruler, but every day he became sadder and sadder and more and more lonely.

Then, one day, there came a huge and fierce dragon which flew in through the castle gates and settled upon the pile of treasure in the great hall. The servants fled down the mountainside, leaving the king and his most trusted minister alone with the terrible beast. They escaped into the highest tower, up a staircase that was too narrow for the dragon to climb, and there they sat and shivered and wondered what to do next.

Both of them knew that it was a waste of time to try to overcome a dragon by sheer force, but apart from that, they found that they didn't know anything. So after some discussion, they decided that they would have to send for help. The first minister was entrusted with the task of seeking out the most beautiful maiden in the kingdom, for it is well known that dragons love young maidens, and can often be influenced by them. So, in the dead of night while the dragon was asleep, the first minister crept out of the castle and down the steep track to the valley.

But the minister found no cooperation among the subjects of the king. For once there was no father or mother who would claim that their daughter was beautiful, because none of them wanted their child to face the danger of the dragon.

So the minister was left alone in the town square. In his misery he sat down on the ground and put his head into his hands. All day he stayed sitting there, because he could think of nothing better to do. As night was beginning to fall, he decided that he would have to go back and report his failure to the king, but just as he was about to stand up, he heard soft footfalls at his side. When he looked up, a lovely young maiden was standing beside him.

'I'm sorry to bother you,' she said, 'but I heard that you were looking for a maiden to try and get rid of the dragon. I know that I am not beautiful, but if you have found no one else, I would like to try.'

The minister stood up. 'Oh, but you are beautiful,' he said. 'In fact you are far too beautiful. I could not possibly take you up there and allow you to face that terrible beast.'

'But I want to go,' said the maiden. 'A year ago I was standing in the street and I saw the king ride past. I fell quite in love with him, and have thought of nothing else since then. My heart is full of sorrow because I cannot be with him, but if you will give me this chance to help him, then my life will never be so empty again.'

The minister looked long and carefully at the maiden. At last he said, 'Very well,' and together the two of them climbed up the mountainside until they came to the castle gates. When they arrived there, they found the king waiting for them.

'I saw you coming up the track,' he said, 'and I remembered that once I saw you in the street when I was riding. I have thought of you often since, and now that I have found you again, I can't possibly allow you to risk your safety by going to meet the dragon. I have decided that I will go in myself and try to persuade him to leave.'

But the girl said, 'It is well known that weapons and men are useless against dragons. I may have little chance, but you have none at all.'

With that she quickly kissed him and darted through the gates into the castle.

By now the heat inside the great hall was tremendous. When the dragon saw the girl, it lifted its great head and said, 'Who are you and what do you want?'

'I am just a girl,' said the maiden, 'and there are some who say I am beautiful. I have come because I have heard of your great fame and power, and I wanted to meet you and see if you would bring me to your home across the seas.'

'I see,' said the dragon. 'They are right, those who say

that you are beautiful. But why should you want to come with me to my home across the seas?'

'Because I have heard that it is a magical place where maidens stay young for ever.'

The dragon sighed contentedly and said, 'Ah, it is, it is. Come a little closer and I will tell you more about it.'

The maiden stepped closer, and as she did so, she felt as though she were beginning to enter a dream.

'Yes,' said the dragon, 'I can take you there, to that place where you will be forever young, and where love never dies.'

She moved closer still, and the dragon's warmth was like the pleasure of her mother's fireside after a long day's work, and his breath was like the scent of summer meadows.

'I will show you a place where all your finest dreams come true, and you can live them again and again. I will show you a place where there is nothing that you cannot do, and nothing that you cannot be. But there is no need for us to cross the seas.'

The maiden stopped and tried to remember. Dimly, she recalled the king's face. 'But we must, mustn't we? We must leave this place to go there?'

'Come closer,' said the dragon. 'Lie down against my heart and I will show you.'

The maiden could hold herself back no longer. She made her way carefully across the mound of treasure and sat close beside him with her back against his side. The great, slow beat of his heart was like the lulling of waves. He bent his neck around her so that she was enclosed in his warmth and bathed by his breath.

'Close your eyes,' he said, 'and you will see all that is yours if you stay here with me.'

She closed her eyes, and the dragon closed his. And there, in the warm darkness, she entered the dragon's world of dreams, where anything and everything is possible.

For three days the king and his minister waited in the tower for the maiden to return. All the time, the king became more unhappy and restless and it was only with great difficulty that the minister prevented him from strapping on his sword and going in to do battle with the dragon. At last they agreed that the only thing they could do was to try and find someone else among the people who could rescue the maiden and rid them of the dragon.

So, in the dead of night, while the dragon was asleep, the minister crept out of the castle and down the steep track into the valley.

There he gathered together all the people from the town and the surrounding villages and told them everything that had happened. 'What we are looking for now,' he said, 'is someone with an idea.' There was silence from the crowd.

'Who can we send?' said the minister. 'There must be someone who will rid the kingdom of this evil?'

Again there was silence. The minister became desperate. 'If we can't find anyone who will offer to help, then the king himself will be forced to take on the dragon. And where will we be without a king?'

The crowd muttered. In exasperation, the minister said, 'Is there no one among you who is willing to face the dragon on the king's behalf?'

Just then, a ragged young man stepped out of the crowd. 'I don't know anything about either half of the king,' he said, 'but I'd like to have a look at that dragon.'

There was a roar of laughter from the onlookers.

'Who is this man?' asked the minister.

'He's just a fool, Sir,' said the Lord Mayor. 'Don't take any notice of him.'

'Shall I ignore him?' said the minister, 'or are you such a nation of cowards that the only champion we have is a fool?'

Still no one came forward. In a rage, the minister took the young man by his torn collar and marched him off up the mountain. At the castle gates, he gave him a push. 'Go on, then,' he said. 'Go and take a look at your dragon.'

'Thank you, sir,' said the fool, and he wandered into the castle.

No sooner was he inside the door than he forgot all about the dragon and fell instead to exploring the castle. The first room that he found was the dining room, where he climbed up on to the long table and danced a jig. Next he found the armoury, where he tried on several suits of chain mail and spent a happy hour playing pick-up sticks with a quiver of arrows. When he got bored with that, he went into the kitchen and fried himself a couple of eggs.

In the tower high above, the minister was trying to persuade the king to abandon the castle and his treasure and move down into the valley. But the king swore that he would never leave the castle until he knew what had become of the lovely maiden. Even as he spoke, he was sharpening his sword. The minister kept on talking, all the while praying for a miracle.

The fool had a snooze on the king's four-poster bed, then poked around in the servants' quarters for a while. He couldn't remember where he was, or why, but he was thoroughly enjoying himself. And the next room he went into was the best yet.

A hall of mirrors.

All the walls, even the backs of the doors, were lined with mirrors. The fool stood on his hands, then on his feet, then on his head until he couldn't remember any more which was up and which was down. In every mirror he looked quite different. In this one he was wise, in this one stupid. In that one he was happy, and in that one, sad. In another one he was huge and powerful, and there was even one where he couldn't see himself at all, although he was sure he must be there somewhere. It took a long time for the fool to get fed up of making faces at himself, but eventually he did. Then he stood in the middle of the room and tried to remember which way he had come in. But each end looked the same as the other. So he turned himself around as many times as he could count, which was three, and headed in the direction he was facing when he stopped. When he opened the door, he thought that he had found the furnace, because a great blast of hot air nearly knocked him down. Then he saw the dragon.

'Oh,' he said. 'I'd forgotten about you.'

When the dragon heard him it lifted its great head, and the maiden stirred in her dreams and opened her eyes for a moment.

'Who are you,' said the dragon, 'and what do you want?'

'No one in particular,' said the fool. 'I was just looking around. What's that you're sitting on?'

'What business is that of yours?' said the dragon.

'No need to be like that,' said the fool. 'Shove off and let me have a look.'

'Get out,' snarled the dragon. 'Get out before I snap you up like a peanut!'

'God,' said the fool. 'You ought to do something about your breath.'

The dragon let out a terrible roar and sent a gust of

flame shooting out towards the fool. But the fool had already ducked back into the hall of mirrors.

'Missed,' he called around the door. 'Where's my peashooter?'

The dragon got up with surprising speed, and his movement wakened the maiden at his side. He snaked across the treasure to the door, where a volley of peas rattled off his snout. In a monstrous rage, he lunged into the hall of mirrors, just as the fool closed the furthest door behind him.

The dragon found himself surrounded by enemies. There is nothing in the world that a dragon hates more than another dragon. Bellowing flame in all directions, he fell into a savage frenzy, snapping furiously at the other dragons all around him. They seemed to be everywhere at once, and all of them coming at him. And they were getting the better of him, because every time he was about to close his jaws on one of them it somehow hit him on the snout, and every time he blew fire at one it blew it right back at him.

Up in the tower, the king and his minister held tight to one another. The floor and walls were shaking so hard that it seemed the castle would fall. In the great hall the maiden saw the dragon lunging around in some awful madness and ran to close the door on him.

Mirrors cracked and crumbled into powder as the dragon destroyed his own images, one by one. At last, with just one dragon remaining, looking him straight in the eye, he paused. So did the other. Then, out of the corner of his eye, he saw the twitch of a tail beside him. With all his speed and all his power he dived upon it and sunk his teeth deep into it. Instantly, he knew that he had sealed his own doom. For, as everyone knows, once a dragon has his teeth into something he can never let it go. So, since it was his own tail that he had caught, he was stuck fast and forced to stew in his own juices for as long as he might live.

When the king came down from the tower to see what had happened, he found the maiden coming out to meet him, and the fool curled up asleep in the broom cupboard.

The king and the maiden were married the next day, and the fool became their chief advisor. Of course, he was never to be found when he was needed, and even when he was found he consistently refused to offer an opinion, but no one could contemplate life in the castle without him. For the castle was very different now. The heat from the captive dragon kept the whole place as warm and snug as a cottage kitchen, and the forests in the valley below began to grow again. Before too long the halls and courts began to resound with the sound of children's voices, and neither the king nor the queen were ever lonely again, as long as they lived.

*Alan Durant*

ROCHEFAULT'S REVENGE

*Illustration by Tim Stevens*

## *Alan Durant*

### ROCHEFAULT'S REVENGE

We were walking down by the old canal when we saw it. There's always lots of junk and rubbish there – rusty bicycle frames, broken pushchairs, gutted umbrellas – but this was different. Someone had dumped it there and it was old all right, but it wasn't junk. It was in perfect condition and it was beautiful: more a work of art than a mirror. A mirror was just an object you looked in to brush your hair or check your spot damage; this was something else. This was the kind of mirror that a gorgeous fairytale princess or a film star might gaze into to admire themselves. None of us had ever seen anything like it before. We stood and gawped.

To be honest, we weren't used to seeing beautiful things. Well, on the box maybe, but not in real life. Our homes were full of cheap stuff mainly. My mum and dad had a painting of a flamenco dancer on the lounge wall that they reckoned was all that, but even I could see it was tat. The kind of thing you might see on a market stall around Christmas time. This mirror, well, like I say, it was something else. It was all elegant curves, decorated with delicate roses and flecked with gold leaf. The wood was dark and polished, without a chip on it. The oval of glass was unmarked too. It was the sort of treasure you'd expect to see in a museum or a stately home, not on the muddy banks of a dingy old canal. No wonder we stood and gawped.

It made me feel good, warm, staring at that mirror. The way I sometimes felt when I saw a really nice-looking girl in the street or when somebody around me did something generous or kind. That was the feeling I got when I looked at that mirror. It was like a moment of rescue, a glint of hope, a sign that life wouldn't always be like this – being skint and bored, hanging out by a stinking, rubbish-strewn canal. I reckon maybe we all felt the same. Even Alex who liked to give the impression that he revelled in the ugliness of his life, who never opened his mouth these days without gobbing some obscenity. Even he was transfixed by the beauty of that mirror.

Entranced, we shuffled closer. We said nothing. We didn't look at each other. Our eyes never wavered from the mirror. And there we were, the seven of us, gathered in awe round that mirror like it was some sort of altar. How long did we stand like that? Looking back it seems like ages, but it was probably only a minute or so. Long enough for me to read the name, Rochefault, lightly engraved at the base of the glass. Long enough to wonder.

Then CRACK! Alex kicked out. Not a hard kick, but enough to crack the glass and break the spell. But why? Why did he do it? He never said and we never asked. Alex did things like that, sudden surprising violent things for no apparent reason, or no reason he could name. No, that's not really the mystery. The mystery is why we, who a moment before had been in the mirror's awe, now turned to its destruction. Alex kicked again, laughing this time, and Tom copied. And suddenly we were all joining in, kicking and laughing, in a riot of destruction. We smashed the glass, we stomped on the wood, kicked and stamped, kicked and stamped, until the mirror smashed and splintered and was nothing but ugly wreckage. A piece of broken, worthless, abandoned junk like everything else there. We fell about, panting and giggling, knocking into one another cheering, weirdly ecstatic, as if we'd just managed some magnificent feat.

What idiots we were.

And me, the biggest idiot of all. I was supposed to be the sensitive one, the artist, 'cause I liked reading books and writing and used big words, and lived in a house that my parents owned, not a flat on the estate like all the others. You wouldn't have expected any more of Tom or his brother Kelvin. They were natural bashers; all they wanted to do was get out of school and join the army. They didn't give a damn about anything. I did. Supposedly. Well, maybe that's why it was me that saw the face. In the midst of all that destruction, I saw it: a face as white as death with the blackest eyes and a look of deep... what? Not malevolence, no, that came later. Anger, accusation, recrimination? No. None of these. It was only there an instant, gazing out through the fractured glass, but I'm sure the expression on the face was one of deep unhappiness, misery. Intense enough that in all the hilarity it made me shiver – though I said nothing. No one would have believed me if I had. Like I said, I liked writing, making up stories. Not that it would have made any difference if I *had* said anything and they *had* believed me. We'd broken the mirror. It was done. The bad luck was out.

It started with small things. Stuff that irked, but you soon got over: losing a favourite possession, a minor injury on the playing field, an exciting opportunity missed. We all suffered a little from setbacks like these in those first few months, but our lives were basically unchanged. Until that summer.

Each year, at the beginning of the summer holiday, the school organised an outdoor, adventure holiday in the Lake District. Tom had been on about it for ages and so had Kelvin. It was just their sort of thing – camping, climbing, canoeing… Mick went too. He was Tom's best friend in our gang and the quietest of us all. You'd hardly know he was around most of the time — yet, well, it's strange, but I think he's the one I miss most. Maybe it's because we talked the night before he went; I mean really talked, just the two of us, for the first time probably. He was on his way back from town, getting some last minute holiday supplies, when I met him. We talked a bit about the holiday and then, suddenly, he said, Do you remember that mirror we smashed up down by the canal? I had a dream about it last night. It sort of came to life, with hands and a face and everything, and started to stalk us. It was weird. He gave a grim kind of smile. There's an idea for a story, he said.

That was the last time I saw him. Three days later, he was dead — Tom and Kelvin with him. They were walking on Scafell Pike when a thick fog suddenly descended. Somehow, Mick, Tom and Kelvin got separated from the rest. No one realized till the main party was down the mountain. Then they set up a search, but visibility was too poor. Next morning, when all was clear again, they found them, halfway down the mountain, stone dead. Even if they'd survived the fall, exposure would have got them.

That night they died, I saw the face again. It gazed out at me from the bathroom mirror, this time its black eyes filled with such malevolence I shrunk back and shouted. When I looked again it was gone, but it haunted my dreams – just as it had Mick's. Next day, the awful news came.

We'd barely had time to come to terms with that tragedy, when a second happened. This time it was Vincent. He was knocked off his bike in a hit-and-run accident. There were no witnesses. A couple out walking their dog found him lying in the road, unconscious. He died in the ambulance on the way to hospital.

I guess I should have known something bad was going to happen. That evening, before I heard the news, the face appeared in the mirror, staring out behind my reflection with a smile of evil intent. It lingered this time, so there was no way I could pretend I'd imagined it.

I avoided mirrors after that. Even shop windows gave me the creeps and I'd quickly avert my eyes from them. I suppose I hoped that if I saw no evil, then no evil would happen. At the back of my mind, though, I knew:

breaking a mirror meant bad luck. Seven years of it, if the superstition was to be believed. Well, seven of us had broken that mirror and no one could have had worse fortune than us that year. It was as if we were suffering a whole seven years' worth of misfortune in one go – sharing out those seven years between us. Maybe now it was over. Maybe. I prayed that it would be so. But I never really believed it.

For a couple of months, nothing terrible happened. I started to regain a little confidence. I even dared the odd glance in the mirror and was pretty shocked at what I saw there. I've never been what you'd call skinny, my face was always well-rounded; well, now it was so gaunt and bony I hardly recognised myself. Hollow-cheeked, baggy-eyed, I looked the way I felt. Well, seeing that jolted me into action. It was time to do something.

I remembered the name, Rochefault, that had been engraved on the beautiful mirror and decided to try to find out what I could about him. I tried the library and the Internet without success and then went to see my uncle, Lionel, my mum's brother, who dabbled in antiques. He wasn't much help, but he put me in touch with a friend of his, Dennis, who was. Rochefault was a celebrated French craftsman, he said, who'd lived in the time of Louis XVI. He asked me why I wanted to know and I told him about the mirror – though not what we'd done to it. I said I'd seen it abandoned down by the canal, but when I'd gone back it was gone.

Describe it, he said. So I did. Are you OK? he asked me suddenly and I realised I was shaking, shivering. Just talking about the mirror was turning me into a nervous wreck. He'd do some research for me, find out more, he said. He told me to come back in a few days.

I slept better that night than I had for weeks. Next morning, I looked in the bathroom mirror and I saw the face.

It was Alex who gave me the bad news. He phoned to tell me Jermaine was in hospital – a football accident. His leg was badly broken. He laughed ironically. Lucky bastard, he said. What do you mean? I queried. Well, he's not sodding dead, is he? Alex pointed out. No, I agreed. But we spoke too soon.

When Alex phoned me back later he could barely speak. He was hysterical, almost incoherent. I had to keep asking him to repeat himself, because I couldn't make out what he was saying. He's dead! he shrieked at last. Don't you understand, Marlon? Jermaine's dead!

There had been complications with his leg and they'd decided to operate. They gave him an anaesthetic – and it killed him. Maybe they gave him too much, maybe it was some freak reaction, but his heart gave out. Jermaine never woke up.

Alex calmed down a little when we'd talked for a while and I asked him about the mirror. It was strange, but, apart from that time when Mick had told me about his dream, none of us had ever talked about the mirror since that day down by the old canal when we found it and smashed it up. Do you remember that mirror, Alex? I asked him now. Yes, he said kind of reluctantly. All this stuff that's happening, all these deaths, I believe it's because we broke that mirror, I said. And I told him about the face I'd seen, was still seeing, and about Rochefault and who he was – well, the little I knew. I saw the face too, he said, which took me by surprise; I'd somehow imagined I was the only one. And I've seen it every day something terrible's happened since, he went on. I can't stand it, Marlon. I can't stand it anymore. And he broke down again. I told him to hang on, that I'd have more information in a couple of days when I saw

Dennis again. The year was nearly done, I said, the bad luck would soon be over. But he didn't believe it and to be honest, neither did I.

That was the last communication I had with Alex.

Two days later, I went to see Dennis, and on the way, I saw the face in the wing mirror of a car, but I hardly broke stride. I was resigned to my fate now. I expected to die, was almost wishing it.

Dennis had found out quite a lot about Rochefault. He was a very successful maker of objets d'art – of highly decorative cabinets and mirrors and other items much prized by the French aristocracy. He had a very high reputation: his work was much-loved by Marie Antoinette, who had commissioned him to fashion a mirror for her dressing room in the Palace of Versailles. Then the Revolution came. It is said, that Rochefault was in the street, putting his precious mirror, finished at last after months and months of labour, in a carriage for delivery to the Queen, when an angry mob appeared. They stormed his workshop, smashing and wrecking, destroying many of his pieces, before torching the place. Rochefault ran in to the workshop to try to save his work – and was never seen again. Just days after, Marie

Antoinette went to her death on the scaffold. What happened to the mirror no one ever knew. It'd be worth a fortune, Dennis said. I laughed at that. Ill fortune, I said, misfortune, not fortune. Seven years' worth. What do you mean? he said. Nothing, I said. Nothing. I thanked him for what he'd found out and left.

They were taking Alex's body out into the ambulance when I arrived on the estate. He hanged himself, someone said. I stepped forward to try to reach him – and I fainted.

There was nothing left for me to live for. All my friends – Tom, Kelvin, Mick, Vincent, Jermaine, Alex – they were all dead. And I was going to die too. But I wanted to meet my nemesis, confront it face to face. I knew more than the others and I wanted a glimpse of understanding before I went. I reckoned I was owed that much. So I went down to the banks of the old canal, where it had all started, a year ago to the day exactly. It was just the same, rubbish-strewn, grubby, stench-ridden, a watery junk dump. The mirror wreckage had gone – the splintered pieces no doubt long since chucked into the stinking water – but shards of the broken glass remained. I gazed at them, prodded them with my shoes, hoping for what I don't really know but...

WHOOSH!

Suddenly, terrifyingly, the face rushed out at me from the mess of glass and, as I fell backwards, it loomed over me, its black eyes huge, terrifying in the midst of the unrelenting, ghostly whiteness. I cried out, petrified, too scared to shake. Rochefault! I whimpered. Rochefault, why are you doing this? The eyes narrowed in a horrible, vindictive smile. You know why, the face breathed in a voice so cold it could have turned the canal to ice. You destroyed my mirror; I have destroyed you. But it was a mirror! I panted. I know it was beautiful and we shouldn't have smashed it – it was stupid. But it was a mirror, for pity's sake. You've destroyed six lives for a mirror!

WHOOSH!

The face zoomed in even closer. You're like that ignorant mob, it hissed. You destroyed beauty on a whim, simply for the pleasure of destruction. There's no greater crime. Beauty is everything. There is nothing in the world greater than beauty. Destroy it and you too must be destroyed. Then go on, kill me! I pleaded, shutting my eyes tight against that demonic vision.

You've destroyed all the others; now, destroy me. My request was met by chilling laughter. Oh, never fear, I shall destroy you, said the voice. Yours is to be the worst luck of all. But your fate isn't to die. I opened my eyes, perplexed, bemused. The face was fading, shrinking; it had almost vanished entirely as its last words swished like an icy mist in the air: Your fate is to live.

*Annie Dalton*

LILAC PEABODY

*Illustration by Sarah Young*

## *Annie Dalton*

### LILAC PEABODY

It's unbelievably early on Christmas Day, but we've been up for ages, putting the final touches to our big surprise.

I do the high-up parts, my little brother Eddie just does as far as he can reach. He's got glitter on his PJs and he can't stop smiling. Once we've finished the actual room, we half drag, half roll the tree from its hiding place.

Eddie almost blew it last night. He banged his head on our bunk beds and started howling. We'd managed to conceal the tree (kind of) but the whole room STANK of pine needles. Dad came charging up the corridor to see what was wrong. Before he could open the door, Eddie bellowed. 'Go away! I want Mitch, not you, Daddy!' So Dad went away again and we sagged with relief.

Decorating a Christmas tree is hard work, a bit like putting tinsel on a hedgehog. Pretty soon we run out of baubles. Luckily, we've still got about a mile of Christmas ribbon, so I fill any spaces with glittery bows.

I let my little brother fix the angel on the top. Then I switch on the twinkle lights. Ta daa! And it's like I've switched on Eddie too. His face shines.

'WOW!' he says. 'Can I open my stocking now?'

'Not until Dad gets up,' I say firmly.

Eddie droops. Dad's still out cold with the duvet over his head.

My dad told us back in November how it was going to be. 'I can just about go to work. I can even pay bills and put food in the fridge, but I can't hack Christmas and I'm not even going to try.'

Maybe you think this is shocking, but I knew Dad

was just trying to survive. We were like three sleepwalkers, just trying to get by the best we could. I'd probably have gone on sleepwalking for the rest of my life. But three days ago something happened and – well, everything changed.

I sound like a total fruit cake, don't I? So let's backtrack a few days and I'll tell you how it all began…

It's the season of goodwill and tacky cotton-wool beards, but where do you think I am? Outside Mrs Cooke's office, that's where. You'd think they'd give me a break, seeing as it's also the last day of term. But I can't do anything right at this school. I just open my mouth and they're down on me like a ton of bricks.

Mrs Cooke calls me in and I get the usual speech. I'm a bright boy, but I have a bad attitude. If I don't change my ways, yadda yadda yadda.

'I mean, why pick on Becky of all people?' she says angrily.

I glower at her. 'I just said girls should stick to girl stuff and leave boys to do the boy stuff. Is that like, a *crime* these days?'

'It's not your opinions we object to,' says Mrs Cooke.

'It's your behaviour. Miss Ainsley says you were extremely aggressive. She says—'

I watch her mouth go yadda yadda, until she finally runs out of steam.

'Oh well,' she sighs. 'When you come back in the New Year, you can make a fresh start.'

'New Year!' I scoff. 'That's just a stupid date on the calendar. It's not like it *means* anything.'

She lets me go and I hurtle down to the childminder's. My little brother waits silently by the door, clutching a home-made Christmas card.

'Better not let Dad see that,' I snap.

On the way home we pass a litter bin and I hold out my hand. Eddie hands over his card and trudges on without a word.

He rarely talks these days. To anyone visible, that is. Though he's constantly chatting to his imaginary mate, Lilac Peabody. (Eddie pronounces it Ly-lick.) He threw a major tantrum when I told him she didn't exist. 'She does, she does!' he shrieked. 'She's all shimmery-bluey-green like a dragonfly.'

'Why's she called Ly-lick then, you birdbrain!' I jeered.

Eddie stopped mentioning her after that.

We've got this huge flat in a converted warehouse. Dad bought it years before warehouses were cool. Our sitting room has views over the river, and there's a street market practically outside the door.

The stall holders are packing up by the time we get home. A bored youth is slinging unsold Christmas trees into a van. All their roots have been sawn off, leaving these pathetic little stumps. And suddenly I can't seem to breathe.

Christmas was her favourite time of year. Dad used to say if it was up to Mum, we'd have more decorations than Oxford Street.

Last year to tease him, she actually hung a glittery mirror-ball in our car. Amazingly Dad didn't take it down.

I saw her reflected in it the last time she drove us to school. Dozens of Zoës, all sparkling back at me. That's Mum's name. Zoë. It means Life, or Happiness or something.

She had us too young, that's why my mum kept taking off all the time. She was trying to catch up on all the fun she'd missed while she was changing nappies and mopping up baby sick.

I've been kidding myself she'll come back in time for Christmas. It's only when I see the trees, that I realise this is never going to happen.

Eddie's seen them too. I can tell from his eyes. And suddenly I'm dragging him along so fast, his feet lift right off the ground. I don't stop even when he starts to cry, just yank him through the market and up to our front door.

'You can forget Christmas trees,' I snarl. 'Dad threw our decorations away, remember? You heard him. Christmas is *cancelled*.'

In a gentler voice, I say, 'Christmas is a *girl* thing, Eddie. From now on it's just three guys doing guy stuff. You'll get the hang of it, you'll see.'

My brother nods like a four-year-old zombie. By the time we reach the lift he's even stopped snivelling. We ride up to the top floor and I unlock the huge stainless steel door and let us into the flat. Eddie silently helps himself to crisps and wanders off to play.

Mysterious rustling sounds come from our bedroom. Eddie must be sharing his crisps with Lilac Peabody. I hear him say wistfully, 'I wish Mitch could see you too.'

And I turn up the volume on the TV.

At that moment, Dad walks in. 'Turn that thing down,' he says in his new tired voice. 'And give me a hand with these groceries.'

When I go to bed, Eddie's already fast asleep. I climb up to my bunk in the dark and find this dense forest of paper chains hanging over my head! *That's* what all the rustling was about. Eddie's totally defied Dad's wishes and put up his own Christmas decorations! He must have made them at the childminder's.

Then all the hairs rise on the nape of my neck, as I see a familiar object shining through the darkness. It's Mum's mirror-ball. Eddie's rescued it from the rubbish and hung it in the window.

I can't leave it there. Dad will go nuts. Yet I can't bring myself to rip it down either. It's pathetic, but I feel like she's still *in* there somewhere. This trashy little bauble is all we've got left of Mum. The only thing.

I get under my duvet and try to go to sleep, but my eyes keep being drawn back to the mirror-ball as it glitters and turns in the warm air. And I start to wonder if I'm dreaming with my eyes open. Something is happening. Mum's little Christmas decoration is giving off an unearthly brightness. The mirror-ball is actually pulsing with light like a star. It grows brighter and brighter until I have to shield my eyes.

I catch my breath, as a child's face shimmers into focus.

I tell myself it's nothing to be scared of. Just a little kid. OK, so it's a little alien kid, with weird designs on her face, but I'm a big boy, I can handle it.

There's a fizzing sound like someone lighting a sparkler. PHITZ! And she's right here in our room, sitting cross-legged on our chest of drawers!

I have time to notice shimmery dragonfly colours, exactly as Eddie described. She looks as if she's on her way to some wild extra-terrestrial carnival. Then Lilac Peabody says calmly, 'Good, it worked.'

I'm still staring wide-eyed. 'Uh?'

'Eddie wished you could see me,' she explains. 'And now you can.' She sighs. 'I've tried to be a good friend to him but it's your help he needs.'

'Oh, boy! I am in BIG trouble,' I mutter. I mean, a thirteen-year-old boy talking to his kid brother's imaginary friend. That *has* to be certifiable.

She laughs. 'You're not crazy, Mitch. You're the sanest person in this family.'

Her expression grows serious. 'But this isn't right. It's three days to Christmas, yet there's no tree, no presents, no Christmas food in the fridge. It's breaking Eddie's heart.'

I clench my fists. 'Leave my brother's heart out of this,' I say furiously. 'Do you seriously think a few Christmas decorations can make up for losing your mother? I don't blame Dad for cancelling Christmas. He's trying to be honest, that's all.'

Lilac Peabody doesn't seem impressed. 'There's being honest, and then there's giving up. Your dad can't get through this by himself. Nor can Eddie. That just leaves you, Mitch.'

To my horror, she starts to fade.

'Come back,' I plead. 'I can't – I wouldn't even know where to begin!'

But she's gone. At least, she's no longer visible. I know she's still around though, keeping up the pressure, because next day I wake up suspiciously bright and early, even though it's the first day of the holidays. What's weirder still, is that for the first time in months I feel almost excited. I whizz back down my ladder like a fireman.

'Time to get up,' I hear myself tell Eddie.

After breakfast we head for the post office, where I draw out every last penny from my savings account. I decide this is more than enough to cover the essentials.

We wander round the market in the wintery sunshine, trying to find a special present for Dad. We eventually decide on a designer baseball cap. We even remember to buy gift wrap. And whenever Eddie's not looking, I buy little cheap goodies for his stocking. I tell myself we're doing really well, you know, for boys. As for Eddie. He hasn't looked this relaxed in months. But on the way home I see his face has gone all haunted again and I sense he's fretting about something.

That night Lilac Peabody beams down and tells me what's bothering my little brother.

'Christmas isn't just about presents, Mitch,' she explains. 'You've got to make everything *look* right, you've got to make it *smell* right.'

'What are you? The yuletide Gestapo?' I complain.

But next day we go to the library where I find a book called *Countdown to a Perfect Christmas* and it turns out she's right. According to the author, we haven't even started yet! We need oranges, cloves, cinnamon sticks, mixed nuts, fancy crackers… The list goes on and on.

'I'll have to rob a bank to pay for this,' I say despairingly. Eddie droops and sighs. 'OK,' I say. 'We'll do the shopping, then I'll make us cheese toasties for lunch, and then we'll really get cracking.'

Making clove oranges is incredibly fiddly. It also kills your hands. We make three, then it's time to get down to the mince pies. I try to tell Eddie not to treat the pastry like play dough but when they come out of the oven, our pies are depressingly lumpy, not gold and puffy like in the book. But Dad's due home any minute so I hastily whisk everything out of sight and open all the windows to let out those giveaway spicy fumes.

That night Lilac pays a lightning house call. She says Eddie's worried I've forgotten the tree…

I smile drowsily, 'It's under control, Peabody!'

'What about dinner?' she demands.

'Sorted,' I yawn. 'Marks and Spencers ready made Christmas nosh. Turkey, stuffing, bacon rolls, little chipolatas. The works. Just trust me, OK?'

'OK,' she smiles. 'Good work!' And she's gone again.

We buy the tree last thing on Christmas Eve. The man is so anxious to get shot of it, he lets us have it for less than half price. He even throws in some decorations for free!

Now everything's ready. And we can't wait another minute. We go to wake Dad. We drag him into the sitting room, still half asleep.

For some reason I'm assuming he'll be thrilled, maybe a little bit proud. His two motherless boys have organised a whole family Christmas all by themselves!

I never dream he'll do what he does, which is to turn deathly white and collapse into a chair. 'But we agreed. We *agreed* we'd cancel Christmas.' His voice shakes.

'I – I know,' I stutter, 'But—'

'You deliberately went behind my back,' he says in the same shaky voice.

I'm a mess of conflicting emotions. I'm terrified Dad will go ballistic. I'm steaming mad. I'm also hurt as hell.

'I don't blame Mum for leaving you!' I want to scream. 'Who'd want to live with a killjoy?'

But I just go numb. I tried, I tell myself bleakly. I did everything Mum would do and it just didn't work. Boys can't do this stuff. It's impossible.

My dad has his head in his hands. The room doesn't look Christmassy any more. It looks all wrong. It looks pathetic. This is probably the worst moment of my entire life.

Then Dad looks up. I realise he's trying to smile. 'Sorry, kids,' he says in a husky voice. 'That took me completely by surprise.'

I feel as if part of me has died. I have no idea what to do or say.

Then Eddie draws a big breath. 'You've got a present under the tree,' he tells my dad in a proud voice. 'And I know what it is. It's a c—'

'Shut UP!' I threaten him.

Eddie gives me a sly grin. 'It's a c-c-cool present,' he finishes triumphantly.

He runs to fetch it.

The lumpy parcel makes me feel ashamed. 'I'm not so good at wrapping,' I mutter.

Our dad unwraps the designer cap. He turns it round in his hands, reads the label, then shyly puts it on.

It looks kind of funny with his bare feet and old pyjamas. We all giggle nervously.

Suddenly Dad rushes off. He comes back with his arms full of green and blue parcels, tied with glittery silvery ribbon. Three for me and three for Eddie. Mum must have bought them before she left.

'I didn't know what to do with them,' he admits. 'I couldn't bear to throw them away.'

I feel sick, scared and happy all at once. I'm desperate to see what Mum bought me. But Dad is still gazing around, totally stunned.

'You even filled a stocking for Eddie,' he says softly.

'There's chocolate coins,' Eddie pipes up. 'And a sugar mouse.'

'You peeked, you little rat,' I scold him.

'I didn't, I felt it in the toe,' he beams.

'You really did this all by yourself?' Dad says.

Me and Eddie exchange glances.

'Kind of,' I say.

And that's how this story ends, with three guys having Christmas together, well, three guys and an invisible girl.

Though I'm assuming Lilac Peabody, whoever she is, has completed her mission because she never appears to me again.

After a few weeks, even my little brother stops mentioning her. But that's cool, because Eddie has real friends now.

And believe it or not, so do I.

*Mary Arrigan*

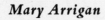

THE DISAPPEARANCE

*Illustration by Tim Stevens*

## *Mary Arrigan*

### THE DISAPPEARANCE

It didn't help that the wind was howling that November evening, and that storm clouds were sweeping across the evening sky like the shadows of galloping giants. And it certainly didn't help that Mum and I were leaving the familiar flowery wallpaper and washing-crowded balcony of our rented apartment to come and live in a nowhere place behind trees and tall grass.

'I think we've made a terrible mistake,' said Mum, wiping the condensation with her sleeve and leaving little bits of hairy wool smeared on the windscreen.

'Too late now,' I grunted. 'Anyway, the neighbours gave us all those going-away presents so we can't go back.'

'Just think, Lucy, I really own it,' Mum said. 'I've never owned anything in my life.'

Which was true. Mum didn't even own herself, she often said. Since my father had died when I was three, she'd been working for a catering company. She was always sloshing things in bowls and stirring yellow mixtures and cleaning the oven. And tired. Always tired.

I remember the expression on Mum's face when we were excitedly trying to decide what to do with our lottery winnings. Not the big win, of course, but there were just enough noughts to make us hysterical. Her face kind of lit up like a light had gone on inside her head, and she pressed her hands together.

'I could run a bed and breakfast,' she said. 'A country guesthouse.'

'Cool, Mum,' I said. 'You could cook for yourself instead of a gang of bossyboots.'

We picked this house from the back of the property pages. A bargain, the estate agent had said. The relatives of the old man who'd owned it lived in Australia and just wanted to offload it as soon as possible. So here we were, with all our dreams invested in a rain-washed Victorian pile.

'It'll be all right, Mum,' I said. 'A few licks of paint and we'll have this place humming. Come on.'

'It's going to take more than a few licks of paint,' she said. 'I knew I should have taken my time, looked around at other places. Look at it now. How will we ever make it respectable enough for people to want to stay here? Anyway, Lucy-light-of-my-life, let's go inside.'

We held hands as we went from room to room. Big rooms with high ceilings and brown furniture. Brown curtains that sent out clouds of dust in the gloomy light when Mum pulled them back. Brown photos of men with collars like those neck-braces you see on people who hang out in the health centre. Brown wallpaper and old, brown air. Was all the world brown before I was born?

Mum 'oohed' and 'aahed' as she went around touching all the fiddly little ornaments on the high mantelpiece and on the dusty shelves.

'Imagine leaving all this stuff,' she said. 'You know, some of these things might fetch a good price. I can take them to one of those posh auction places in the city. We could make enough to buy paint, curtains and even wallpaper. We can do this, Lucy! We can make this guesthouse thing really work.'

'Wicked, Mum,' I laughed. 'It looks brighter already.' Which it did. And so did Mum. Sometimes your dreams just need a little nudge to help make them real.

Upstairs we picked the biggest bedroom to leave our things.

'All masculine stuff,' Mum said. 'Easy known there was no woman in the house. The poor old dear was a bachelor. No wonder the place is a shambles.'

She pulled open a drawer and bent down to look inside. She took something out of the drawer and laughed. 'A tortoiseshell mirror!' she exclaimed. 'How pretty. Must have belonged to some ancient aunt.'

She pushed back her hair and held up the little hand mirror to look at herself. It was discoloured, just like everything else in this house, and had little shiny things on the frame.

'A tight corset, Mum, and you'd look like a Victorian lady admiring herself,' I joked.

We lit a fire in the big bedroom, made tea and unrolled our sleeping bags because we weren't sure about the beds. Mum put some drops of lavender on our pillows to help us sleep. But it didn't help her because I heard her sighing a lot. So it mustn't have worked for me either. At least not until the deepest part of the night when I dozed off, thinking about how Mum and I would manage to turn this brown and dusty house into a place where bouncy tourists with big shorts and back-to-front baseball caps would come for sunshine and bacon and eggs. It must have been while I was dozing that Mum disappeared.

I wasn't frantic at first that morning. Downstairs I pulled back the wooden shutters in the long sitting room and let the morning sun push its rays through all the brown. At least last night's rain had blown itself out, making the house slightly more cheerful. I stood at the bottom of the stairs and shouted up.

'Mum! Mum!' My voice just echoed back. The dust danced eerie shapes in the sunlight. 'Mum, stop playing creepy games and say something.' But the dust simply danced new steps to my voice.

She must have gone out. But when I tried the front door and the back door, they were both bolted from the inside. I dashed about frantically trying the windows, but they were as firmly locked as when we'd checked them last night. I crept back along the passage leading to the kitchen. The faint scrape of a chair on a tiled floor lifted the cloud of worry off my head, and I laughed at myself for being a wimp.

'Where have you been?' I shouted, pushing open the creaky door.

'I beg your pardon?'

It wasn't my mother who was sitting at the table. It was a boy with a flat cap and trousers that met his socks at his knees. A boy who looked like he fitted in with all the brown around us.

'Who are you? How did you get in here?' I shouted so that I wouldn't sound scared. 'This is private property. My mum and me own this house. You'd better get lost, sunshine.'

'Where is your mother?' the boy asked rudely, looking at me from head to toe.

'She's…' I stammered. 'That's a stupid question. Now

you'd better go before she comes down. She's huge and she's been on Gladiators loads of times.' That was the sort of fib that appealed to me.

'Your mother has disappeared, hasn't she?' the boy said, taking a mouthful of milk from the carton we'd left out the night before because the fridge was scummy. He wiped his mouth with his hand and looked at me. 'That's why I'm here.'

I squeezed my fists really hard because my mind went all funny.

'What do you mean?' I asked. 'Where's Mum?'

The boy stood up.

'I have to tell you a story,' he said in a funny accent.

'You're crazy!' I said. 'I don't know who you are, with your stupid clothes and daft cap, but you'd better tell me where my mum is or I'll punch you one.'

Someone had once told me that if you're really scared you should act extremely tough and the scariness will go away. That proved to be totally wrong because, even though my face was screwed up and my fists were waving, I was as scared as I could be.

'Hush. Calm down,' said the boy. 'My name is Alastair. I was Australian. I've come to help you.'

'Was?' I gasped. 'Are... are you dead? A dead Australian?'

The boy called Alastair nodded. 'Trust me,' he said when I started to gabble and cringe, as you would when you find yourself talking to a dead person from a foreign country. Funnily enough, when he touched my arm I wasn't so scared any more. He didn't seem like a ghost. Anyway scary ghosts wouldn't wear flat caps and silly trousers that meet their socks at their knees. 'Listen to my story,' he went on. 'It is an Aboriginal legend.'

I frowned. 'What's this got to do with my mother?'

'Patience,' said Alastair. 'It's about a tribe called the Spiny Lizards. One day a man called Wayamba came to their camp and stole a beautiful woman. He took her back to his own camp and his people were angry because the Spiny Lizard tribe would come looking for the woman and there would be trouble.'

I couldn't see the point in listening to a story like this when my mum was missing, leaving me in a brown house that I would never be able to run as a guesthouse on my own. But I pressed my lips together to stop the words coming out. You have to be polite to people who come all the way from the past to help you.

'That very day,' went on Alastair, 'the Spiny Lizard people came for the woman. But Wayamba was ready for them. He came out of his hut, wearing a shield that covered his front, so their spears just bounced off him. Then they tried to attack him from behind, but he was wearing a shield on his back too. When they tried to clobber his head which was poking out of the shields, Wayamba ran to the river and swam away. The Spiny Lizard people put a curse on him. He was turned into a creature encased in a shell, with just his head sticking out.'

'Serve him right,' I said. 'He shouldn't have nabbed that woman. He should have sent flowers first, or something.'

Alastair smiled. 'Well,' he continued, 'the shell of that creature became very precious to the Spiny Lizard people. It showed that nobody could interfere with their ways and go unpunished. Everywhere they went they always took some shell with them.'

'Fine,' I said. 'Very interesting story. Now I must go and look for my mother, thank you very much.'

'But that's the whole point of the story,' said Alastair. 'It's because of that shell that your mother is missing.'

'Huh?' I said, sitting down because my knees wobbled.

'That's the whole point,' said Alastair again. 'My father was friendly with some of the Spiny Lizard people. They gave him a piece of the shell. But they warned him it must never leave Australia, that if even a piece of the shell leaves Australia, the first woman to touch it will disappear to avenge the woman Wayamba kidnapped.'

'So?' I said.

Alastair nodded. 'My father had it made into some kind of an ornament. Then, a few years later, his cousin, James – the late owner of this house – came to visit. My mother, who didn't know about the warning, gave him the ornament, said that it might be useful if he ever wanted to give it as a present to a woman. But he never did. It is here, and your mother must have touched it. Unless we find it and get it back to the Spiny Lizard tribe, she will never come back.'

'Do you know what this ornament thing is?' I asked when I was able to form words again.

'No,' said Alastair. 'I'm afraid I don't.'

'Well, that's a big help,' I said. 'I would have thought

that ghosts would know pretty much everything. What's the point in coming all the way back from... from the dead if you don't know a simple thing like that?'

'Look, I've been sent because I'm the same age as yourself,' he said. 'They thought I could help you sort things out. We don't just go round being clever and knowing-all-things out there, you know.'

'Out where?' I asked.

'You don't need to know,' said Alastair. 'Now, do you want my help or not?'

A mind-flash told me to hold on to him. Ghostly help is better than none when your mum is missing.

'Sorry,' I muttered. 'Where will we begin?'

'We have to look for anything made of shell that your mother might have touched.'

'She touched millions of things,' I groaned. 'Anyway, how will we know it if we find it?'

Alastair smiled. 'I'm Australian, remember,' he said. 'There's just one thing,' he added. 'We have to find it by dusk or it will be too late.'

Once again my knees wobbled, but as I was sitting down I didn't fall in a heap on the floor. 'Oh cripes,' I whispered, trying to picture Mum's face in case I never saw it again. 'What exactly will happen at dusk if we don't find that shell ornament?'

He bit his ghostly lip which didn't look at all ghostly, 'I'm afraid they'll come for you too,' he said.

'What?' I tried to swallow, but my throat wouldn't work. 'Why me?'

'It's all to do with the legend,' he said. 'First they take the woman who touched the shell. Then they'll take her nearest loved one.'

The blood in the top of my head drained right down to my shoes.

'Come on then,' I said, leading the way to the sitting room where Mum had been looking at all the fiddly ornaments. We had about four hours before the winter dusk. There were dozens of things that Mum could have touched. They could have been made from shell or play-dough for all I knew.

'We're only looking for things made of shell,' said Alastair, as if he read my mind. Which was extra scary because your head should be a very private place.

'This is hopeless,' I said.

'I'm getting tired,' said Alastair. 'I need food.'

I remembered that he'd been drinking milk when I

first saw him, but a ghost looking for grub?

'I never heard of a ghost wanting food,' I said.

'How many ghosts have you met?' asked Alastair. 'The thing is, when we come back across we're just like we were. We get hungry just like you. Now, let's make a sandwich or something. I haven't had a sandwich since 1941. And that's the one I choked on.'

We went back to the kitchen and made thick sandwiches from the bread and cheese that Mum and I had brought. I sliced the cheese really small so that Alastair wouldn't choke again. I wasn't sure if people could die twice or not.

Alastair leaned over and touched my arm again. 'We'll find that shell,' he said. 'It's here and we'll find it.'

But we didn't find it. We rummaged in every room, but there seemed to be nothing made of shell.

By the time we got back to try the sitting room again, the sun was beginning to sink, just like me. When the clock began to chime a quarter to four, we heard the distant babble of voices. I looked at Alastair and I was horrified to see that he was beginning to fade.

'They're coming,' he said.

'Who?' I cried. 'Who's coming?'

'The ancient spirits,' he said. His voice sounded like it was coming from far away. 'The ancient spirits of the Spiny Lizard people. They're coming for you, Lucy.'

'For heaven's sake, Alastair, don't go fading away on me,' I cried.

'I can't help it,' he said. 'When they come, my time is up.'

I pulled out every crummy ornament within reach. But it was no use. Those voices were getting closer. 'Are you sure it was shell?' I screeched.

'A shield of shell,' his voice was almost an echo. 'Shell in front and shell at the back, with only his head poking out. Wayamba turned into a creature covered in shell.'

A *creature covered in shell*. And then it dawned on me.

'A creature covered in shell,' I shouted. 'With just his head sticking out. A tortoise! We've been looking for the wrong bloomin' shell, Alastair. We should have been looking for *tortoise* shell. And that's the last thing Mum did. She found a tortoiseshell mirror and she was dancing around with it!'

I dashed up the stairs two at a time to the big bedroom where Mum and I had spent the night. I could hear Alastair's boots behind me, but I didn't stop to see if the rest of him was coming too.

I pulled back Mum's sleeping bag.

'It's not there!' I cried.

'Try inside it,' said Alastair. 'It might have slipped down inside.'

I reached in frantically, conscious of the babbling voices that seemed to be on the stairs.

'I have it!' I shouted. 'The tortoiseshell mirror.'

With one sweeping movement Alastair grabbed it and went out of the door.

All this stuff was very bad for my health. I sat on Mum's sleeping bag and hugged my knees. The sudden silence was heavy with expectation.

'Alastair?' I called softly. Still no sound – that is until there was a loud knocking sound from downstairs. Surely ancient spirits don't usually knock on doors, I told myself. Could it be that my dead friend had forgotten how to pass through closed doors? What to do? I couldn't just go on sitting on my Mum's sleeping bag forever, so I crept down the stairs, squinting my eyes in case there might be an ancient one left over and lurking.

'Alastair,' I called again.

'Lucy!' a muffled voice came from a door under the stairs.

Mum's voice? I was almost afraid to open the door in case she wouldn't be there and I'd start to blubber.

'Mum!' I yelled, tugging at the stiff door. 'You're back. Oh, you're back!'

Mum looked at me in amazement as I threw myself at her, squeezing her waist really hard to check that she was solid.

'Easy on there,' she laughed. 'I must have fallen asleep in this airing cupboard. I came in here to look for some extra blankets. When I woke up, I couldn't open the door. Thank goodness you heard me. I was getting quite claustrophobic. Look at the time,' she went on. 'I've slept for almost the whole day. I can't imagine what came over me to be so exhausted. I'm still tired.' She took a deep breath and put her hand to her head. I hadn't the heart to tell her that she'd been trekking to Australia with a bunch of ancient ones.

I didn't want to leave her alone in case she might disappear again, but I told myself that was silly. All the disappearing business was over, now that the ancient spirits of the Spiny Lizards had got their tortoiseshell mirror.

I ran back upstairs to find Alastair. I searched every room. There was no sign of him. That is, until I found the small boomerang that had been left on my sleeping bag. Boomerangs come back, I thought. Some day, perhaps, Alastair would come back too.

*Berlie Doherty*

THE GIRL OF SILVER LAKE

*Illustration by Sarah Young*

## *Berlie Doherty*

### The Girl of Silver Lake

This is the story of a girl who fell in love with a fish. But it wasn't an ordinary fish. And she wasn't an ordinary girl. She was a girl who didn't want to grow up.

She lived by a lake in a beautiful valley. Sometimes the lake was busy with boats; yachts with butterfly sails, speedboats with water-skiers towed along behind in white wings of spray, launches full of waving tourists.

But at other times the lake was so quiet that she could hear the water breathing, and that was when she loved it best.

When she was very young she used to play on the shores of the lake, paddling and swimming, skimming pebbles to make them bounce across its surface. When her father had finished his work in the hotel kitchens he would take her out in his old rowing boat. What she loved was to be right out in the very middle of the lake. Then her father would paddle with just one oar so the boat turned slowly round in a circle.

Now she could see how the lake, too, was like a circle. Like a round mirror. The trees and mountains seemed to turn themselves upside down into it.

'The world is under the water!' she laughed.

'No,' her father said. 'What you can see is a reflection of our world.'

She understood what he was saying and yet she understood something else too. Deep inside herself she felt that the mirror world of the lake *was* the real world. But she said nothing of this to her father. She didn't tell him how happy she felt when she looked down over the side of the lake and saw her own face reflected there. Her long hair draped down from her shoulders and floated like strands of reeds on the surface. She let her fingertips sip the water, and when she lifted her hand out the water drops slipped away as if they were threads breaking. At times like this she knew that she was part of the water and that the water was part of herself.

'I want to see the world under the water,' she said dreamily.

Her father laughed. She thought how strange it was that grown-ups didn't understand these things. That was why she didn't want to grow up.

And then, one day, she saw the fish and fell in love with it. Of course, she had seen many fish before. She had seen them leaping for flies on summer evenings. She'd seen them in little silvery shoals, clustered together and flowing through the water in the way that flocks of birds drift through the sky. She had seen the shimmering catch her father brought home sometimes in the bottom of his boat.

One day she went out in the boat on her own. If her mother and father had known, they wouldn't have let her go; she knew that. The lake was deep and dangerous. It was so wide that a boat would be lost from sight before it reached the other side. And sometimes, because it was surrounded by mountains, it harboured thunderstorms. She knew all that, and yet when her parents were busy one day in the hotel she took the boat out and rowed as far into the middle of the lake as she dared. She shipped her oars and waited, letting the lake's silence sing to her.

A fish leapt from the water. It flashed with such brilliance that she cried out for it to leap again, but the water was calm except for the ring of ripples the fish had made. They spread out into wider and wider circles until they lapped against the side of the boat, making it rock gently. At last the water settled and lay perfectly still. Yet she could see that there was a glittering circle on the surface of the water where the fish had risen and sunk.

She dipped her oars in and paddled slowly towards the circle, careful not to break it. Now she could see that the circle was made of small bright iridescent flakes like floating stars. And every one of them reflected her face.

Without thinking twice about it, she scooped up as many of them as she could and tipped them into the bottom of the boat. There they lay like the tiny pieces of a broken mirror, smiling up at her as she smiled down at them. She wanted to wait and see the fish again, but it was growing dusk, and a pink light stole over the water. She must go home.

She moored the boat on the lake shore and gathered up the glittering fragments in her hands. She ran into the cottage near the hotel.

'I've found something wonderful!' she shouted. 'Come and see! I think they might be stars that have fallen out of the sky.' She opened her hand to show her mother, but the jewel flakes had turned dull and brown in her palm.

'Fish scales!' her mother said. 'What's wonderful about fish scales? Throw them away, child.'

The girl couldn't believe what had happened. But she didn't throw them away. She took them up to her room and threaded them on to a piece of cotton and wore them round her neck all night. But in the morning she hid her necklace inside her dress so no one would see it and make her throw it away. All she could think about was the beautiful fish, and she longed to row out on to the lake and look for it again, but the chance didn't come. She stood by her window, watching the lake, hoping for a sign of the fish. For three days the lake lay like a sheet of white glass.

And then her mother noticed a strange thing. The girl had shiny flakes like the scales of fish on her arms.

'What have you been doing?' she shouted. She bathed her daughter and scrubbed her skin, but nothing she did could remove the scales. She found the necklace, which the girl had hidden under her pillow, and threw it into the lake.

'Keep away from that water,' she warned her.

But the girl couldn't get the leaping, brilliant fish of Silver Lake out of her mind. Next day, when her parents were busy she went out in the boat again. As she rowed, the scales on her arms gleamed and flashed in the sun, and she smiled to see them because they were beautiful. She rowed right to the middle of the lake again, where the mountains formed a perfect circle round her and plunged their green arms into the water. She shipped the oars inside the boat and waited. The sun grew cold, clouds gathered in the sky, and still she waited.

She saw many fish leaping for flies, and heard the *plash*! as they sank into the water again. But there was no sign of her mirror fish or the ring of jewels. The light began to grow dim and soft like pearls, and she knew that she should leave. And then, just as the first stars bloomed in the sky, a fish leapt out of the water in a gleaming arc. Everything was reflected in it: the silver speck in the purple sky, the deep blue of the mountain tops, the watery glow of the rising moon. And then the fish sank into the water, leaving a ring of ripples which grew wider and slighter until all that was left was a circle of floating jewels.

Quickly the girl dipped her oars down and rowed into the circle. She leaned out and saw her face reflected in a hundred different ways in the mirror scales. This time she left them in the water. She knew them for what they were, and she didn't want to drain away their light and their life. But as she looked down at them she could hear the ripple of water all around her, and it was as if it was washing over her, as if she was inside the lake instead of peering into it.

During the night there was a thunderstorm. The girl stood at her open window and looked out at the black sky and the lightning forking through it as if it was trying to rip it apart, and she thought of the beautiful mirror fish. She closed her eyes and felt the swish of chopped water around her. She heard the rain drumming above her on the lid of the lake.

'What are you doing, child? You should be in bed.' Her mother led her away from the window and pulled back the covers of her bed. Just as the girl climbed in, there was a mighty flash of lightning that lit up the room, and in the white light the mother saw what her daughter had tried to hide from her. Her body gleamed with the scales of a fish.

'You must never, never go on the lake again. Do you hear me?' her mother demanded.

But how could the girl say yes, when every bone in her body ached to be swimming under the black water with her mirror fish?

As soon as her parents were asleep the girl crept out of the house and ran to the lakeside. Her father had filled the boat with rocks, but she had no need of it now. She waded into the lake, up to her ankles, up to her thighs, and when the water lapped against her breasts she knew that she was no longer a child. Joyously she plunged down and down. Reeds stroked her. Little fishes swarmed around her. She turned over and over in her element. The water was like silk streaming across her flesh. In the moonlight she saw how her body gleamed, and how beautiful it was. Her mirror fish swam with her, twisting this way and that, leaping with her into the soft rain.

When morning came, her father and mother stood on the shore of the lake, looking for their daughter. They were frantic with worry. Rain sliced round them like silver arrows. The mountains breathed white mist, and Silver Lake was as grey as ice.

'Our child has gone,' the mother cried, and a hush fell across the lake. The mist cleared, the rain stopped. Grey drained away from the sky like smoke and the blue of day poured through. The colours of the mountains reflected green, dun, amber, purple into their own perfect images. There was a holy silence on the water.

The man and woman gazed around them in wonder. They had never known the lake to be so still, or to take the colours of the world into itself so perfectly. Even in their grief for their lost child they wondered at its beauty.

Then they saw the fish leaping into the air. They saw the colours of the mountains and the trees and the sky reflected in it. 'How beautiful!' they gasped. The fish made a perfect shimmering arc. As it dipped towards the water the jewel scales fell away from it and there stood their daughter, a young woman in all her beauty. She waded towards them and stood watching with them. The circle of mirror scales spread out around the mother and father and their daughter in a perfect ring, and sank down into the dark, quiet mystery of Silver Lake.

# ABOUT THE AUTHORS

**MARY ARRIGAN** was born in County Kildare, Ireland and now lives in the countryside of County Tipperary. She studied art in Dublin, won a travel scholarship to Florence University then taught art for eighteen years. Mary began writing short stories for magazines and radio and is a frequent broadcaster on RTE radio. She has written and illustrated picture books for younger children and novels for older children and teenagers. Mary won The Sunday Times/CWA Short Story Award for *The Song Went Up the Stair* and the Hennessy Literary Award for *Backyard Majesty*. She won the International Young Library (Munich) White Ravens title for her teenage novel *The Dwellers' Beneath* and a Bisto Merit Award for the picture book *Siuloid Bhrea* (A Grand Walk).

**MALORIE BLACKMAN** was a database manager and systems programmer before becoming a full-time writer. *Hacker* won the W H Smith's Mind Boggling Books Award and the Young Telegraph Children's Book of the Year Award. *Thief* won the Young Telegraph Children's Book of the Year Award and *Pigheart Boy* won an UKRA award. A.N.T.I.D.O.T.E won the Stockport Children's Book of the Year Award. Malorie Blackman won the Excelle/Voice Readers Children's Writer of the Year Award. Other novels include *Dangerous Reality, Whizziwig,* which was made into a popular BBC Television series, *Jack Sweettooth the 73rd* and *Tell Me No Lies*. Her most recent book is *Noughts and Crosses*. Malorie lives in Kent with her husband and their young daughter.

**MELVIN BURGESS** was a trainee journalist, a casual labourer and a dyer of silk before making a career out of writing novels. His first book *The Cry of the Wolf* was published in 1990. His other titles include *An Angel for May*, *The Baby and Fly Pie*, *The Earth Giant*, *Kite*, *Tiger Tiger*, *Burning Izzy*, *The Copper Treasure* and *Bloodtide*. His latest book is a novel based on the film *Billy Elliott*. He won the Carnegie Medal and the Guardian Fiction Award for *Junk*. Melvin was born in London, brought up in Sussex and Berkshire and now lives in Manchester.

**ANNIE DALTON** has worked as a waitress, a cleaner, a factory worker and is now a full-time author. Her book *The Afterdark Princess* won the Nottinghamshire Book Award. *Night Maze* was shortlisted for the Carnegie Medal as was *The Real Tilly Beany*. *Naming the Dark* and *Swan Sister* were shortlisted for the Sheffield Children's Book Award. Other books include *The Dream Snatcher, Out of the Ordinary, The Alpha Box* and a new series, *Angels Unlimited* which arose out of a short story written for the anthology *Centuries of Stories*. Annie was born in Dorset and now lives in Suffolk.

**BERLIE DOHERTY** was born in Knotty Ash, Liverpool and now lives in the Derbyshire Peak District. Her serious writing started at university where she was studying to be a teacher. She has twice won the prestigious Carnegie Medal, once for *Granny Was a Buffer Girl* – in which there was a whole chapter based on her parents – and once for *Dear Nobody*, the playscript of which won the Writers' Guild Award. *Daughter of the Sea* also won the Writers' Guild Award. Her other books include *The Snake-stone, Street Child, The Sailing-ship Tree, Tough Luck, Spellhorn* and her newest novel *Holly Starcross*.

**ALAN DURANT** is a copywriter for a children's publisher as well as being an author. His books for teenagers include *Blood, Publish or Die* and *The Ring of Truth*. His stories for younger children include *Little Troll, Spider McDrew, Creepe Hall*, the Leggs United and Bad Boyz series, and picture books *Big Fish, Little Fish, Big Bad Bunny* and *Hector Sylvester*. He has twice won the Kingston Borough/Waterstones Poetry Prize. Alan was born in Sutton, Surrey and lived in Oxford, Paris and London before settling in New Malden with his wife and three children.

**ANNE FINE** was born in Leicester and taught for a while before becoming a full-time writer. She has won many awards including the Carnegie Medal twice: for *Goggle-Eyes* which also won the Guardian Children's Fiction Award, and for *Flour Babies* which also won the Whitbread Children's Novel Award. *The Tulip Touch* also won the Whitbread Children's Novel Award. *Bill's New Frock* won the Smarties Book Prize and *How to Write Really Badly* won the NASEN Book Award. Anne won the Publishing News Children's Author of the Year Award in 1990 and again in 1993 and became the second Children's Laureate in 2001. An adaptation of her novel *Goggle-Eyes* has been shown by BBC Television and her novel *Madame Doubtfire* was filmed as *Mrs Doubtfire*. Anne Fine has two grown-up daughters, and lives in County Durham.

VIVIAN FRENCH worked in children's theatre for ten years before she established herself as a storyteller. In 1988 she began to write for children and has written numerous books since then. Highlights include *Caterpillar, Caterpillar* which was shortlisted for the Emil/Kurt Maschler Award, and *A Song for Little Toad* which was shortlisted for the Smarties Book Prize. Books for younger readers also include *Morris the Mouse Hunter* and *Guinea Pigs go to Sea*. For older children she has written *Aesop's Funky Fables*, *Kickback* and under the name of Louis Catt, two novels in the Sleepover series. She has travelled from Orkney to Oklahoma talking about children's books, is a visiting lecturer at the University of the West of England, and reviews for the *Guardian*.

GAYE HİÇYILMAZ grew up in Surrey and has lived in Turkey and Switzerland. Her novels often revolve around young people who are forced to undergo extraordinarily difficult circumstances in many areas of the world. Gaye won the Writers' Guild Award for her novel *The Frozen Waterfall* and has been shortlisted for the Smarties Book Prize, the Guardian Children's Fiction Award and the Whitbread Children's Book of the Year. Her other novels include the highly acclaimed *Girl in Red* and *Flame*. Gaye Hiçyilmaz has four grown-up children and now lives in Pembrokeshire, West Wales.

LESLEY HOWARTH grew up in Bournemouth and now lives in Cornwall. Her first novel, *The Flower King*, was shortlisted for both the Whitbread Children's Book Award and the Guardian Children's Fiction Award. *Maphead*, won the Guardian Children's Fiction Award and was Highly Commended for the Carnegie Medal. She was joint winner of the Smarties Book Prize for *Weather Eye*. Reviewing her novel *Mister Spaceman*, Philip Pullman noted that 'Howarth is superb at conveying the ordinariness of the odd, and the oddness of the ordinary.'

ELIZABETH LAIRD was born in New Zealand of Scottish parents. She has lived and worked in Malaysia, Ethiopia, Iraq and Lebanon and now lives in London with her husband. Elizabeth has a special interest in Africa and travelled all over East Africa to research her *Wild Things* series. She has a long-term love for Ethiopia and has journeyed to every corner of the country, collecting folk stories from traditional storytellers. Some of these have been published in *When The World Began*. Of her novels, *Kiss the Dust* won the Children's Book Award and

*Hiding Out* was the winner of the Smarties Young Judges Award. *Red Sky in the Morning* and *Secret Friends* were both shortlisted for the Carnegie Medal.

**CELIA REES** was born and brought up in Solihull, Warwickshire. She was a teacher of English and History for many years and started writing as a direct response to her pupils who liked exciting stories, thrillers and chillers! Her books include *Truth or Dare*, which has been on several shortlists including the NASEN Awards, *Soul Taker*, *The Cunning Man*, *The Bailey Game*, The Haunts series and the highly acclaimed *Witch Child*. Celia now lives in Leamington Spa, Warwickshire, with her husband, Terry. Her daughter, Catrin, is currently at university studying Law.

**PAUL STEWART** was born in London. He studied English at Lancaster University and Creative writing at the University of East Anglia with Malcolm Bradbury and Angela Carter. He has written more than forty books for children – from picture books to fantasy and horror for older readers. *The Wakening* was one of the Federation of Children's Books Group 'Pick of the Year' books. *Beyond the Deepwoods*, the first title in the Edge Chronicles written in collaboration with illustrator Chris Riddell, was shortlisted for the Lancashire Children's Book Award. Paul lives in a tall thin house near the coast with his wife, Julie and children, Joseph and Anna.

**JEREMY STRONG** has been a headteacher, teacher, caretaker, strawberry picker and a jam doughnut stuffer! His first book was *Smith's Tail*, published in 1978. Since then he has written many books including five stories about *The Karate Princess*, and the books about Nicholas and his family of which *My Mum's Going to Explode* is the latest. His three Viking stories – *There's a Viking in my Bed*, *Viking at School* and *Viking in Trouble* – have been made into a hugely popular television series. Jeremy Strong won the Children's Book of the Year Award for *The Hundred-Mile-an-Hour Dog*. His work is characterised by its humour and direct child appeal. Jeremy was born in Eltham, South East London. He now lives in Kent.

**KATE THOMPSON** was born in Yorkshire and lived in London, New York and India before becoming a resident of Ireland. Kate writes poetry as well as novels for children and adults. Her acclaimed trilogy for children *Switchers, Midnight's*

*Choice* and *Wild Blood* received many accolades as has her novel *The Beguilers*. Her latest novel *Only Human* is the second title in the trilogy *The Missing Link*. Her adult novels are *Down Among the Gods, Thin Air* and *An Act of Worship*. Kate Thompson currently lives in County Galway with her two daughters.


## ABOUT THE EDITOR

WENDY COOLING is a highly-respected and well-known children's book consultant and reviewer. She taught English in Inner London comprehensives for many years before becoming head of the Children's Book Foundation (now Young Book Trust) where she initiated the Bookstart project, now being implemented nationwide. She is a regular guest on radio and television programmes and is the compiler of many anthologies, including *Centuries of Stories* also published by Collins.


## ABOUT THE ILLUSTRATORS

TIM STEVENS was born in the heart of Epping Forest and has only ever wanted to draw. He had to wait until he was at art college before he knew it was called illustration. He thinks working as an illustrator is the best job in the world. One week he can be drawing backward-speaking tortoises or wizards and flying carpets, the next sharks with moustaches and monks with smelly feet. Whenever he is drawing he knows it will be with a smile on his face. Tim went to Camberwell College of Arts and now lives in Suffolk.

SARAH YOUNG works mainly as an illustrator for design companies and book, card, music and magazine publishers. Her work ranges from simple graphic logos to colourful, elaborate paintings. She co-founded a puppet theatre with Jon Tutton and from this grew a business making 3D works and prints – lino and screen – which are exhibited in galleries across the British Isles. Her interest in myths and fairy tales pervades most of her work.